THE CHOICE OF WEAPONS
RAOKE GANG
BOOK ONE

ALEX VALDIERS

https://valdiers.com/dl/

Copyright © 2023 by Alex Valdiers

All rights reserved.

No part of this book may be reproduced in any form or by any electronic or mechanical means, including information storage and retrieval systems, without written permission from the author, except for the use of brief quotations in a book review.

Cover illustrated by Luka Brico. Cover development by thisisreallychris. All rights belong to Alex Valdiers

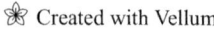 Created with Vellum

THE CHOICE OF WEAPONS

The Red Fleet, composed of Eastern European and Asian soldiers, is the last organized fighting force coming from Earth. The United Forces of the West have collapsed, but the Red Fleet keeps up with the belligerent Cykens and the AI-powered humanoids Huuri for the domination of the galaxy. They are humanity's last hope, but despite their many winnings, the end of the conflict seems further and further away. With the outcome of the war appearing out of hand, two officers of the Red Fleet have been known to hate each other and engage in fighting whenever their paths cross. Their duels across the war zone and the years have quickly become a legend in the army.

This is the story of their feud.

SPRING

*T*he day he met Squall Miura Izuna, Satoshi Ren had taken a solitary stroll through the rocky hills of Ahktokhi. He climbed to the highest rock and kneeled, like a falcon scouting the terrain for its next meal. Ren didn't have to scout; he knew exactly where his prey were. They filled the horizon line, thousands of Huuri troops, marching, building, deconstructing, and doing whatever half-humanoid half-machines did.

What a mess.

To human eyes, especially those born into the discipline of samurais like Ren's, the Huuri's activity was nonsensical. They may have had the upper hand in numbers and firepower, but their strategy to occupy the flat ground of the rocky valley was either a stroke of genius or utter stupidity.

If only we had the tools to take the fight to them. Look at that dust—they wouldn't even see us coming. The hooves of mechanical units roamed the valley like wild buffalo, raising blinding clouds of dust in their wake. High on his rock, some three kilometers away from the Huuri camp, Ren could hear the low buzzing of machines at work if he listened closely enough. He had heard that sound before, not in battle but back on Sepunde, where he had infiltrated a Huuri camp to free a group of high-ranking officers of the Red Fleet, consisting of three Squalls—special units answering only to Central Command—and two Domions, the highest commanding officer of the regular army. It was the mission that saw Ren promoted from Sanjo to Domion. The sweet memory of the glorious mission supported by the distant buzz cast an idyllic, treacherous veil over the current situation. The Red Fleet was losing ground. So far, the Red Fleet had accomplished nothing but shedding their troops. If they didn't come up with a better tactic or receive a large influx of new troops and material, the battle for the Arunbaal system would be lost.

We're going to lose the Arunbaal system.

Ren brooded over those words and their meaning.

Central Command won't be pleased. And what? What would that really change for me? If I survive, I won't be demoted. My stock would take a hit, but soon I'll be back in command of a regiment, on some other system, against another army, be it Huuri or Cykens. Really... win or lose, what difference does it make? The Red Fleet won't be wiped out in a day, neither will the Huuri or the Cykens. I'm just a tool in this conflict, a player who would never reap its rewards. The war will be won or lost without me, so what's in it for me? I like fighting. I prefer using my katana when I can, which is rare. I fight, I win. I rise within the ranks of the Red Fleet, proudly branding the banner of humanity.

"The banner of humanity! That's a potent carrot Central Command feeds us with." Ren spoke into the rising wind, a dusty wind that filled his mouth with dirt. Ren twisted his neck to the side to expectorate the dust. Perhaps it was fate in this instant that directed his spit onto Squall Miura's boot, and fate that had brought Izuna to Ren's resting rock.

Izuna watched the brown saliva dripping from her toes

with consternation. A flurry of emotion rushed within her: anger, indignation, surprise, humor. With great control, she forced herself to pick the latter.

"I take it you're planning to clean my boot now, Domion?"

Even after spitting on her boot, Ren hadn't noticed the presence of the Squall who came from the west, where the sun was slowly setting. Squinting to read the Squall insignia on her shoulder pads, he sprang to his feet and mumbled a feeble excuse. It was barely intelligible.

"*Nihon-jin desu ka?*"

Ren confirmed he was indeed Japanese and saluted his senior officer in due deference.

"Let me give you a piece of advice, Domion. If you are ever going to criticize Central Command, do it in your own tongue, not in Russian. Too many of our soldiers would happily hang a dissident Japanese."

"Thanks. Thank you, Squall. Should I… should I be wary of you?"

"Do you mean, 'Am I going to denounce you to Central Command'? No. I won't. This might be the Red Fleet, but we Japanese need to stick together. They are so few of us left." She noticed the katana sheathed at Ren's waist. "Are you sword-trained, traditionally?"

"*Hai*. I was taught from the age of five with Master Ohno from Hokkaido."

"Is this where you're from?" Izuna asked, and when Ren nodded, she told him she was from the Tottori Sand Dunes. "I am a child of the desert myself. This landscape, it reminds me of home. Except, of course, without all those AI-powered soldiers swarming us."

"I've never been to the Tottori Dunes," Ren said without much interest. He kicked a small rock at his feet and watched it fall off into a crevasse. Izuna took offense at his distraction and decided to leave the conversation.

"It's nothing special," Izuna said, flicking her heels and starting her way down toward the camp. "I was glad to escape it, and now look where we are." She stopped and pronounced the next words in Japanese, in a tone filled with innuendos. "Look where Central Command sends me."

When she was halfway down the rocks, under the mesmerized gaze of Ren, she spoke once more, in plain Russian, to warn the Domion about the upcoming small council on the hour, telling Ren not to be late.

REN COMPLIED. He followed Izuna down the rocky path back to camp. He was unwilling to disappoint her and miss his duties, but when he got to the small council at 1800, she was nowhere to be seen. The council started without her. Ren shook his head in disbelief.

Satoshi Ren was the youngest of the five Domions around the small council table. He was also the least experienced, military-wise, but Domions Kurtchef, Arinsky, Nephazin, and Kugai all listened attentively to his idea of retreating to a canyon and setting up a temporary defense base.

"I've lost seven more Qibings in the last skirmish on the plains. The Huuri's flying ability makes it difficult for our troops to guard against. I think we need to narrow the Huuri's angle of attack. If we take the battle to the canyons and organize our defense with air cannons, we can force the Huuri to fight us head-on."

"We can plant k-mines in the canyon," said Domion Nephazin, using his index finger as a highlighter to indicate the k-mines' location on the map laid out in front of the council. "K-mine it, I should say."

"What if the Huuri bomb us from above the canyon? We

would be trapped," said Domion Kurtchef without malice or ill-intent.

"We need to set up our cannons before we move our troops in. We rig the canyon's edges with anti-air cannons, and we… how many cannons do we have?" Ren looked up at Domion Kugai for an answer.

Kugai was staring at the top layer of the tent, only half listening, his arms crossed over his chest, swinging on the back feet of his chair. Ren's direct question to pull him into the conversation took him aback. He nearly fell off, spreading his arms wide to stabilize himself, exposing his embarrassment for all to see. Domion Nephazin sighed disdainfully, but Kugai was prompt to catch up and make allusions that he had been fully invested in the conversation the entire time. "Fifteen, maybe more. Everything is still in kit, we haven't touched it yet. I can't say for sure. Maybe we can build fifteen or sixteen, seventeen."

"Fifteen will do," said Ren, leaning over the map. Domion Nephazin was still tapping his fingers at random points inside the canyon. "We occupy the canyon from here to here," he said, establishing a 600-meter perimeter. "We'll alternate cannons on each flank, fifty-meter intervals."

"If we retreat to the canyons, we all die," said Squall Miura, popping her head inside the command tent. "The Huuri will burn us to a crisp."

"Squall Miura, it's agreeable you have joined us," said Domion Kurtchef. "As we discussed in the first twenty minutes of this council meeting, we can establish secured defenses around the canyon."

"I didn't come all this way and lose this many Qibings to play the turtle. I say we push on through the plains and take the fight to the Huuri."

Ren's initial surprise at the absence of Squall Miura boiled down to annoyance at her lack of apology and the curt way she imposed her views upon the council. Like a wounded lover, his response was one out of spite rather than reason. "At this stage of the battle, with our limited resources, we'll lose many more Qibings if we fight head-on in the open. This would be the wrong approach."

Ren's opposition unsettled Izuna. She had come in expecting to find an ally in her compatriot, not an objector. "We push on, we hurt them. We cower away in this canyon, we risk getting everyone killed for no return."

Ren stood his ground and maintained his opposition. "Not if we organize our defenses well."

"Who talks about defenses? Who are you to talk such nonsense with the lives of so many Qibings in the balance?"

Ren refused to answer. He ground his teeth and stared coldly at her.

"Domion Satoshi is young in age, but his talent on the field has proven equal to the most experienced of our Domions," interceded Domion Kurtchef, holding on to his chair from below the seat as if he was about to fall off. Despite his strong words of support for his young fellow officer, his eyes read panic. Izuna discarded his presence altogether. Instead of answering, she stared at Ren with grievous eyes. In the flurry of emotions boiling within, this time she picked anger. Cold anger.

Ren sustained her gaze and spoke no more words. His silence did nothing but fuel Izuna's anger. The tension in the command tent was palpable.

"I agree with our Squall here," said Domion Arinsky with his characteristic clumsy manner of speaking. "These Huuri here don't like to be hurt. If we focus our present fire on the key-key elements of their attacking arsenal, we can, I'd say, and not with circumvolution on my imagination, but feasibly break their line and blitz through their stock defenses and march on their here army."

"March to where? We don't know how deep their line is."

By the end of the council meeting, the decision to retreat to the canyon was voted through by four to two. Squall Miura made several arguments about advancing across the plains, but ultimately she could not convince Domions Kurtchef, Nephazin, and Kugai to side with her. Izuna did not distinguish between field battles and council arguments. She left the meeting angered by the feeling she had lost a battle, and there was nothing she hated more than to lose. Refusing to let go, she waited for Domion Ren outside the tent, a hand on the hilt of her katana. Ren had a reluctant yet sturdy look on his face that told Izuna he didn't want to eat whatever she was about to serve him.

"Japanese are supposed to stick together, you know? Haven't I said that before?"

"We're not Japanese here. We are Red Fleet officers." As he spoke, Ren held the pommel of his sword and flung it from side to side as if he were helming a ship through a storm.

Izuna ran her eyes from Ren's katana to his face. "You shame me. You are a coward and your fear, your weakness, is so tangible it has infected the other Domions. You do not deserve to be a leader of this army," Izuna said, drawing her sword five inches out of its sheath.

"You insult me and threaten me. You are positively mad."

"On the contrary, I might be the only sane person here." Thus saying, Izuna drew her sword and challenged Ren to a duel.

"What are you doing? You can't be serious. I'm not going to fight you; this is madness."

"Why? Do you think the small council's impunity protects you? You have shamed me, and I demand reparation. Now, draw your sword."

Resignation fell upon Ren. There seemed to be no way out of this duel. "Not here," he said.

"Now!"

"Not here! Not in the middle of camp, in front of our troops. You might be mad, but I am not. We will duel, but not in the open."

Izuna re-sheathed her sword. "Very well, then. Meet me in that precious canyon of yours in a half-hour. I'll show you what a dangerous place it is to take a fight to."

THE CANYON WAS two miles from camp, and although the Huuri forces were on the other side of the valley, Ren could not help but worry about a surprise Huuri attack as he ran to it. Two Qibings accompanied him to act as seconds, both trained as medics. Confident in his sword skills, Ren did not expect to lose this duel, but he assumed that blood would be drawn, his or hers. Fighting a woman did not factor in his mental preparation for the duel. The best fighting instructors he had known were women; most of the Qibings under his command were women. Although he was conscious that, not a century ago, the Japanese code of honor would not have allowed him to draw his sword upon a woman, times had changed. If the Galaxy war had done one good thing, it had been to bring about the end of nepotism and sexism. People were judged upon their merit. The son or daughter of a lord was not guaranteed command; most of the high officers of the Red Fleet were the children of indigent folks, as he was, as was Izuna, but Ren ignored it. Either way, it did not matter to him. The only thing that bothered him was her rank. As a Squall, she was higher in command. If he were to kill her by accident, he knew he might face disciplinary actions, maybe getting court-martialed. As such, he relied on the two Qibings by his side. Their testimony would be his defense. As Ren entered the canyon, he had no doubt in his mind that he would end up victorious.

Squall Miura was already there, and she had brought her entire regiment with her, all 12 of them. They formed a half-circle around Izuna, who sat cross-legged on the dusty ground. She had adopted a meditating pose, her katana laid flat on her knees, eyes closed.

"We fight until one or both of us are incapacitated," she said, remaining immobile.

"We're not doing first blood?"

"Not if we can still fight. I assumed you'd relinquish the prospect of a traditional sword duel?"

"Assume away," said Ren, grabbing the hilt of his katana.

No more words were needed. Ren's seconds stepped aside. Someone said a prayer in Russian. The two duelists unsheathed their swords and adopted a dueling stance. Ren held his katana with both hands, at waist level, inclined toward his right hip. Izuna held her katana above her head with one hand. In traditional Japanese dueling, there was no need to give a top, or say '*hajime'*. The duel started when the first opponent made the first move. Sometimes this could take several dozen seconds, up to a minute. On this instance, it took half that time for Ren to launch the first attack, with an upper slash that he broke halfway through to stab forward and close the distance. The change of stance mid-combo surprised Izuna, who dodged with her body by side-stepping rather than with her blade. She instantly found herself off-balance, her sword position off. Ren lunged at her and hit her with a shoulder charge, which he swiftly followed with a rising sun attack. First blood was drawn. Ren's katana cut into Izuna's flesh at her ankle and grazed off her left shoulder, tearing off her uniform pads.

Unwilling to wound his opponent more than was necessary, Ren did not follow up his attack. Instead, he retreated five steps to safety. Izuna cursed, her teeth drooling saliva like a rabid wolf. She put her weight on her left ankle. A gush of blood tainted the gray dust of the canyon's soil.

"Can you continue?"

Ren hadn't finished his sentence when Izuna was already upon him. She had shifted her position to rest on her right foot, attacking Ren with one arm, in a flurry of horizontal slashes traveling from head to toe. She was fast and gaining speed. The first 10 strikes had been easy to parry, but the attacks soon came faster and heavier. Ren didn't know if he was tiring, but he felt the hilt of his katana trembling in his hands after each strike. This was unusual. He tightened his grip and lost some of the mobility.

In front of him, Izuna was not tiring. She kept hurling at him. And now the slashes slipped through Ren's defense. One strike hit the ground in between Ren's feet; another cut his uniform under his armpit but missed the skin. Ren wanted to counterattack, but he couldn't match her speed. So he began retreating, using his body movement to dodge the sword, thus giving his arm a rest. He backtracked, but Izuna kept coming at him, furious and relentless, leaving a small trail of blood behind her.

Fueled by adrenaline after conceding first blood, Izuna eventually gassed herself out. Her arm tired, she ran out of breath and, from one blow to another, her speed and strength were halved. She gave Ren a window to counter, but the Domion missed it; he too was tiring. His mind had shifted to defense. Instead of striking the Squall at her open ribs, he waltzed two meters to safety, out of range of Izuna's subsequent attacks.

"I can see," Izuna started, breathing heavily, "that retreating comes naturally to you."

Ren had shifted to Izuna's left. When she readjusted her position, she found herself betrayed by her slashed ankle. Her left leg buckled as soon as she put weight on it. Like a wild deer, Ren sprang to his feet and lunged a half-moon attack, with the tip of his sword going from behind his head to the opponent's navel. Izuna reacted, but too late to get a good parry. She deflected Ren's attack but did not manage to break its stride. Ren's blade hit Izuna's collarbone and slashed her skin all the way down to her left breast.

With this attack, the battle was won. The duel was over. Izuna's katana slid through her fingers. She put a knee down. Blood spurted out of her chest. She was hurt, but she did not feel the breath of death upon her, only the sealing shadow of shame engulfing her. In the space of one hour, the proud Squall Miura Izuna had lost two battles to a young Domion from her homeland. From that point on, it would be easy for Izuna to confuse her real enemy for her fellow officer of the Red Fleet: Domion Satoshi Ren.

SUMMER

*I*n the days that followed this first duel, the Red Fleet battalion established their defense perimeter inside the canyon and used scouts to lure the Huuri. Flattened by the shame of her defeat and her physical mutilation, Izuna took no part in the fighting. Day after day she watched from the inside of her tent as Domion Satoshi Ren's plan took the better of the Huuri, who came crashing into the Red Fleet's hands like flies on sticky paper. By the end of the first week, 17 Huuri had been captured; eight of those had a salvageable AI-brain post-death. This harvest of rare technology was a success beyond the small council's expectations. It was agreed that those AI-brains should be transported back to the Red Fleet's nearest base on Sesta VII for analysis. Squall Miura stepped up to command this mission. This time the decision was not taken to a vote.

Ren watched his newfound enemy leave the planet Ahktokhi with an equal dose of relief and apprehension, because he had no doubt in his mind that Squall Miura would one day come to seek her revenge. And now he had to live with the fear of stumbling upon her, wherever he went— wherever the Red Fleet sent him.

. . .

FEAR, it turned out, was a powerful ally for Ren. Fear is a primal emotion that defines what it is to be human—to be alive. Throughout the course of a single life, a person's relation to fear will differ, based on one's personality, health, possessions, entourage, and love. There are times in a person's life when running and hiding from fear is the only viable option. In fact, this is the majority response to handling fear. Very few people hunt down their fear; very few people challenge themselves to best their fear. There was such a time in Ren's life when he believed the old idiom that what doesn't kill you makes you stronger. Lose or win, he believed he would always benefit from dueling with Izuna. And so, he actively sought her to confront her.

As a Domion, his liberty was restricted. Although high-ranking officers, they were bound to go on specific missions in a given sector to lead hundreds, sometimes thousands, of Qibings. Unlike Squalls, who picked their missions and went all over the Galaxy, wherever there was fighting to be done, Domions were consigned to one task at a time, and sometimes those missions lasted months or years. The Arunbaal system was six worlds large; Akthokhi was only the first port of entry. After months of victorious battling on Akthokhi, the Huuri refocused their forces on the fifth planet: Azakhi. Domion Satoshi and his regiments followed. Fortunately, Squall Miura did too. She and her small elite troop of hand-picked Qibings came in dribs and drabs. She would be here for a week, help scout an area, raid a Huuri advanced post, then the next day she'd be gone, on a different mission somewhere else in the universe, leaving Ren anxious for her return. Every time they met, Izuna and Ren dueled. This was the summer of Ren's life as a Red Fleet officer.

. . .

THE RED FLEET had the upper hand on the Huuri, and although they experienced losses, Central Command constantly supported the army flanks with fresh troops. Dozens of Squalls came on a monthly basis, some for support, some to run their own secret missions. Some stayed to fight with the regular troops, some went. There was one Squall who stayed with Ren almost throughout the entire campaign on Azakhi. He was a man named Téchiné— Alexis Téchiné. At 55 years old, he was the oldest Squall Ren had ever met. His skin was riddled, and he was thin and tired-looking. Big bags permanently resided under his eyes. Half the bones in his body, it seemed, had been replaced by metal and resin. When Téchiné spoke, he was always calm and composed, like he had all the time in the world, even in the heat of battle. Some of the Qibings thought he was crazy; Ren thought him brilliant. He had this great father aura about him that fascinated the man from Hokkaido. Often they spoke at night by the senior officers' bonfires. Téchiné knew more about humanity and its history than Ren ever would. He was of an unsuspecting type who appeared shy at first but really was quietly outspoken, never raising his tone, never dropping a conversation. At first, Ren thought he was a madman. He had asked him a simple question, but that question had been used so often it had long lost all meaning. The question was, "How are you?"

"I am terrible," Téchiné answered with a candid and wide smile that hit Ren like an electroshock. He wasn't trying to make conversation; he was walking by, saluting a fellow officer as society's rules dictated he should. Nobody was fine, everyone was getting by, but society imposed a pretense on everyone's greetings. Téchiné didn't. And yet, as Ren would quickly find out by sitting with him to engage in a deeper conversation than he had ever intended to indulge himself in,

Téchiné was doing much better than nearly everyone around the camp.

"Sometimes," Téchiné continued, "I need to pause and look at the world around me, I mean really look, with my eyelids open wide and my pupils cleared of pretense and the blur of comfort."

"Comfort?" The word bugged Ren and alerted him. At the feet of the two men there was a squashed scorpion-like endemic insect, just as deadly, and the anti-bug squad bustled about to secure the officers' bonfire from other dangerous and deadly insects and animals. Ren had stepped on the squashed scorpion inadvertently. A purple viscous fluid stuck to Ren's heel; his legs were covered in dust. "I'll have to say, I've known better for comfort."

At this point, Téchiné reached out for a brand and used it to poke the embers in the bonfire. "Then I am sorry for you," he said, with a touching kindness that convinced Ren to sit down with the man and share his dinner with him by the bonfire. "I see comfort as a veil. Ignorance's greatest weapon. Comfort is the principal casualty of great minds. Sometimes I think about the progress humanity could have made if comfort never existed, and it's maddening. It's like Orson Welles said in *The Third Man*, Switzerland enjoyed 500 years of peace, and what did that give them?"

"I don't know," answered Ren, who didn't get the reference, and frankly ignored who this Welles was.

"The cuckoo clock," Téchiné said with a theatrical grandeur that bore its effect on Ren. "Take Russia, one half of the Red Fleet, the Motherland of many of our Qibings. Unforgiving mother with a poisonous tit, who gave birth to many of humanity's greatest minds: Tolstoy, Leiretzina, Dostoevsky, Ashinova, Tarkovsky, the father and the son, Chekov, Marinova, Pushkin, the Strugatsky brothers. How? By suppressing comfort. Tarkovsky made *Nostalghia* and *The Sacrifice*, his best films, in exile; Strugatsky's best novels *Roadside Picnic* and *It's hard to be a God* were released illegally before passing censorship. Ashinova wrote her greatest music in prison. And Pushkin? Pushkin almost never finished anything he ever wrote. His *Onegin* is missing many stanzas; his greatest novel, *The Moor of Peter The Great*, has only an opening chapter. Comfort is what stopped him from writing —from developing his mind. Comfort is the enemy. But Pushkin was blind to it. And when he lost it—when he lost his comfort, in the form of his young wife, Natalia, seduced by a French man—he tried to recover it by dueling the French soldier. He died, wounded from this very duel. If you ask me, and this is all conjecture on my part, Pushkin wanted to lose that battle; he wanted to die the death of a poet, having given his best verses in a time of dissension and direct opposition with his tsar. Pushkin wanted to die in that duel. I am convinced of this. Are you?"

"Am I? I... I don't know about Pushkin?"

"I'm not talking about Pushkin," Téchiné said, retiring the brand from the bonfire. Its tip was orange with heat. "I'm asking about you. Do you want to die in a duel with Miura Izuna? I've heard you've fought four times in the last two months. I don't know this Squall Miura, but I am interested. What is this compulsion to duel? Why keep butting horns with another officer and risking your career—your life?"

"I don't risk my life. We don't duel with gunblasters, only our swords."

"Yes, because blades have never killed anyone, that's a known fact," Téchiné said with a magnanimous tone, devoid of mockery.

"I don't know if I can put words to our duel, my duel with Squall Miura. I've never thought twice about it. I have to do it. That's what I feel when I see her. And obviously she feels it too, because she's never refused me a duel. She must feel the same too, in a way. I think, yes, we have a connection, in that matter. Dueling is good. Dueling is what we have to do. I need it, and I know she needs it too. It's… this life we lead, you, me, her, them, as officer and soldiers of the Red Fleet, it's so… organized, secluded. Pointless at times, I feel. I don't… control anything." Ren unconsciously grabbed the brand out of Téchiné's hand and began poking at the embers, gently, daring not to anger the bonfire and flick fire shards around it. "Central Command sends my battalion to a star cluster, I go, fight, and stay as long they tell me to stay. I don't make that choice. The Huuri or the Cykens attack us. I attack back. Again, it's not a choice. If I don't, I end. It's not a choice, not a real one. Fighting Izuna... Dueling Squall Miura is a choice. It's something neither Central Command nor the Huuri or the Cykens or any human or element in the universe commanded us to do. It's… I can't explain clearly. It's what we chose. I want to go that way, and no one—nothing—can stop us, for this five, ten minutes the duel lasts, from walking to that duel to the last blow being dealt. Nothing can stop us. It's what we want. It's what we chose, perhaps the only thing we've ever done in our life that we truly did freely. Liberty. It's liberating. We eat because we must, we sleep because we must, we serve the Red Fleet because we must, but Izuna and I don't have to fight each other. Yet, we do. It's… very abstract, and it might sound astounding to you, but I think I'm only truly alive when I duel Izuna. Win or lose, I win. I live. Five minutes at a time. And it's good to live."

"It is good to live indeed. What you are saying isn't abstract to me at all. It's a fact known and discussed for many centuries. Ingmar Bergman, in his film *Autumn Sonata*, has a character say how she only truly lives through her art, but she feels dead when she really has to live her life."

"I am not an artist, just a professional killer," Ren said, letting go of the brand.

"You are Japanese, right?"

"I am," Ren answered, pushing the brand out of the fire awkwardly with his foot.

"Isn't sword fighting one of Japan's ancestral arts?"

Ren looked away, showcasing hints of frustration and annoyance. Téchiné interpreted his reluctance to define himself as an artist as modesty.

"Humility? It's a rare gift. One I admire. I am, myself, a total hubris of a human being, you wouldn't believe. In fact, admitting that I am not humble is truly the only modest thing about me. I am a great man, with a great mind. And I'm fine with the idea, as heavy as it is to carry. All I have to do is stay away from comfort—because comfort, my boy, is the real killer of the mind."

"I thought it was poverty."

"What is poverty? Do you know? I don't. Not anymore. That's where the irony lies. I joined the Red Fleet to flee poverty, and now all I do is flee comfort."

"You are hanging on a middle ground."

"I don't. I go where life is. Most of the time, life escapes me, but eventually, once in a while, I get my own five, ten minutes, when having dinner by a bonfire, dead scorpions all around me, their stinger still pointing at me, daring me to reach for them beyond death, I meet a stranger like you, who has the kindness to open himself. Isn't this special? To have a genuine conversation, once in a lifetime?"

ONCE IN A LIFETIME, Ren dueled Izuna under the sun, five or six times, at repeated intervals, always stopping at first blood to avoid serious injuries that could put any future duels in contention, and worst, make them inapt for service. This was a time of mindless battles sparked by life-enhancing duels. This was the summer of Ren as a Red Fleet officer. Like all summers, it had an end. Squall Miura rode into the sunset to another cluster of the Galaxy, where the Red Fleet waged war on either the Huuri or the Cykens.

FALL

*I*t would be two years before the duelists were reunited. Domion Satoshi gave a year of his life to ensure the total domination of the Arunbaal system. The Red Fleet rewarded his tactical prowess with the rank of Squall, the highest rank attainable by fighting officers. Now he was Izuna's equal in grade. With this new promotion came what Ren would soon realize to be "the illusion of freedom," As a Squall, Ren was now free to pick his troops and his destinations, but he also answered directly to Central Command, whose private orders were somewhat obscure. All the missions Ren undertook in his first year as Squall were run with a hidden objective. Most of the time, Ren ignored whether he had been successful at all. Central Command was not interested in sharing results or greater plans with its field officers.

The nature of the missions varied from the ordinary, like raiding an outpost, to the nonsensical, such as destroying feeding lines between two Red Fleet bases. Squall Ren carried out his orders to the letter, no matter how counterproductive they appeared to be. Oftentimes during those strange missions, he thought about Izuna and his initial dislike of her. He hadn't understood her suicidal approach to fighting back on Ahktokhi and deemed her crazed with a lack of tactical awareness, but now that he was a Squall himself and experienced life as a free-floating high officer, it seemed to Ren he might have misjudged Izuna. The possibility that her orders back then had been different than the Domions' was growing increasingly plausible.

As time went by, the memory of his triumph over Squall Miura, both diplomatically and with the sword on their first encounter, was increasingly tainted by reasonable doubt. It had been easy to see himself as a righteous victor when he thought Izuna was a brash and irresponsible officer, but the perspective that her decision to force the troops into suicidal skirmish after suicidal skirmish was not hers cast a looming shadow over Ren's self-assurance. Rather than the opposition between a rational and benevolent mind and an irresponsible and impulsive ego, his first duel with Izuna might have simply been the result of a clash between two contradicting forces answering to the same ideal.

Needless to say, Ren's nights were growing increasingly shorter as he grew within his Squall outfit. There were sleepless nights when he secretly wished he had never risen within the Red Fleet's officer ranks. He watched the Qibings serving under his orders. Their lives were so simple. They fought, they traveled, they rested. They took simple and clear orders from their line officers, Sanjos, the equivalent of sergeants. If the Qibings ever disagreed en masse, the command decision was taken to a vote that could overturn the order. Such was the way the Red Fleet operated at the lowest level. Everything was diplomatic and communal. But the top of the pyramid operated differently. As a Squall, Ren was isolated from all, even his fellow officers of the same rank. He was a slave to command decisions that were beyond him. This was far from what was promised to him when he joined the Red Fleet. This was not the life he dreamed of.

No matter where he went, which bench of the Galaxy he temporarily rested his backside on, no matter what Central Command asked of him, Ren felt trapped in an invisible cage. This feeling of constant reclusion was having a negative impact on his personality. He was more abrasive, sometimes self-assertive, and less patient or inclined to listen to the opinions of others. The very nature of being a Squall in the Red Fleet was eating at his core, transforming him into somebody he did not want to be.

"Is this who you want to be?" he asked himself in front of the mirror, time and time again. Yet, he did nothing to change, nothing to go against the tide. He was a Squall. Squalls executed the highest orders. It was an honorable position. *Honor is all I have left,* he repeated to himself.

SQUALL MIURA ENDED her summer with a series of dashing victories led on the outskirts of Red Fleet space territory. Every time she conferred with Central Command, she requested combat, rather than running errands deep within the Red Fleet lines. Her chest wound had long healed, her collarbone had mended, and she now bore only a thin rectilinear scar cutting her left breast into two unequal halves.

If word had gone out of her initial demise against a younger Japanese man back on Ahktokhi, it did not transpire within the rest of the Red Fleet. Qibings paid her respect wherever she went, Sanjos bowed before her, and Domions listened and executed her directives more often than not. But the wound had only healed on the surface. Not one day passed that she didn't think about Ren. When she ran the tips of her fingers over her scar, she felt her repressed raging pain, as if all the shame and anger she had felt that day after the duel had been sealed and sewed back deep inside her body.

There had been many duels after their first encounter, but the two duelists had resolved to stop at first blood. Sometimes she'd had been the one to draw first blood, and other times it had been Ren, but none of those duels matched the intensity and flavor of their first encounter. To her, it was almost as if all the other duels did not count. She wanted to pay back Ren for the hurt and the humiliation he had inflicted on her, and she had failed.

For two years, Izuna ran through life with a heavy heart, desperate to get retribution. Yet she never mentioned his name to anyone and ignored all comments regarding her rival. She did not for one second wish to read the empathy in other people's eyes when they thought of Ren and how he had bested her. She knew she would not be able to stand it, so she kept quiet about Ren. She never told anyone how much her body burned to confront Ren once more, but this time engage in a traditional sword fight where the first blood rule couldn't save either of them. Every time she boarded a transporter, every time she entered an outpost or a camp, every time she set foot on a space station, she wished that he would be there: Satoshi Ren, the man who had taken away her pride. And pride was the foundation upon which her character had been established. Without this base, Izuna roamed the Milky Way on rubbery legs. Her self-confidence was dented, and her quick-thinking process slowed drastically, dangerously at times; her personality had been robbed of its colors. Only the blood of Cykens or the severed wires of the Huuri brought her satisfaction and made her feel whole.

So, Squall Miura killed and killed and killed. She built a grotesque reputation as an intrepid and fearless fighter that she openly mocked.

"If only those who talk knew that fear is my main source

of energy, that I am driven by fear," she would sometimes say to a trusted soldier.

"What fear?" this person would irremediably ask.

And Izuna would answer, "The fear of dying incomplete, without my best half."

In her eyes, her "best half" lay in the palm of Ren's hands, wherever he may be. Only toppling the hilt of his sword under her blows would free her missing self and make her whole again. How she longed for it… and how she struggled to contain herself when she heard a familiar voice, that day on Nena Prime Station in that overcrowded cafe. And when she rose above the crowd of drinkers, she locked eyes with the man from Hokkaido. In a few months since their last meeting, he had changed a lot. His hair was longer. His face had become wider and darker. He looked like a man who carried the fate of the Galaxy on his shoulders. His eyes were small and glum, but when he recognized Izuna, they lit up with a spark.

Ren quietly rose to his feet. Both duelists faced each other through a crowd of thirty Qibings and officers. They stared at each other in silence, without surprise or fear, despite the long months of dread and the constant threat of an impending duel that had hung over their heads those last two years. Izuna boiled with eagerness and pure unfiltered joy, while Ren remained calm. Coolly, he sat back and commanded the attention of the drinkers at his table.

"Any of you ever bear witness to a duel?"

The conversation halted, and the three soldiers around Ren considered him gravely. One was a Domion whose name Ren ignored; the other two were Sanjos who had served under Ren's command on a number of occasions.

"Over there sits an old acquaintance," said Ren gravely, "whose only desire is to run her sword through my skin."

"Squall Miura? Is she here?" Sanjo Tsyukova sprung to

her feet, scouting the horizon in the direction Ren had indicated with a head tilt.

"You've heard of her, Sasha? You know about our duel?"

Sanjo Tsyukova lowered her gaze like a naughty dog being reprimanded for climbing on the kitchen table. "I do. We've... we've all heard about your duels back on Arunbaal."

"It's been some time. Yet I knew this wasn't going to be the end of it. I've always known." Ren drained his beer and pushed the glass away as if he was saying goodbye to alcohol for a very long time. His body was rigid, and his jaw bones moved awkwardly under his cheeks; there was a sense of dread, the sense of an ending that the onlookers could not comprehend, not even Sanjo Tsyukova.

Ren's eyes contemplated Sasha and her dashing red hair sitting beside him. She had the small and lithe body of a contortionist. She had allure and had been a coquette as long as he'd known her. Even in the heat of battle she wore makeup, black eyeliner with blue shades, and crimson nail polish matching the roots of her hair. She had the same look Ren had blatantly ignored every time he met with her.

Sasha oozed affection and desire for Ren. In this instant, he felt that if he asked her to stand up and murder Squall Miura in front of the entire cafe, she would have done it without hesitation. For him. But that would be wrong; it would rob Ren of the adrenaline that had kept him going all these months. Seeing Izuna had the effect of a potent drug on him. He felt possessed by fate, intoxicated by the illusion of grandeur. At last, they were going to duel, and this time they were off-mission, free to unleash the wolves from the cage.

"Would you be kind enough to..." He hesitated and forced a smile onto his lips. "... set up a *meeting* with Squall Miura?"

Sanjo Tsyukova stood up immediately without asking for further instructions.

"The earlier the better," Ren added before she left to confront Izuna.

A MINUTE LATER, Sasha was already back. She was rigid, her voice devoid of dynamism. Her brief exchange with Squall Miura seemed to have robbed Sasha of her characteristic enthusiasm.

"She will meet you at 0600 tomorrow. Wherever you wish, she said." Sasha's voice was sharp and rushed, as if she spoke out of anger, but Ren took no notice of her demeanor.

The interest of the Domion at their table was piqued. He carefully threaded his way into the conversation. "Should we check out a shuttle and set up the duel on the nearest planet? I can certainly do that? If that's… If you think that…"

"There's no need to leave the station," said Ren, an air of impatience about him. "There has to be some cargo bay or deserted corridor we can use."

"I heard the rep-p-pair works," said the Domion, stumbling on his words, "on the third dome have been suspended for a week. I could perhaps arrange access?"

"Fine. Just make sure to tell *her*," Ren said, standing up abruptly. "I'm going to call it in. Thanks for the drinks."

Sacha's face quickly shifted from anger to show distress. "Wait, I'll walk with you." She had one of those characteristic visages devoid of all emotional filters. When Sasha was upset, her commissures formed a cross with her arched eyebrows. When she was happy, her rosy cheeks flared up and her eyes scintillated. As one would have guessed, she was a terrible liar.

Ren and Sasha left the cafe together. Ren didn't look back Izuna's way, and when Sasha dared a peek, she only saw the back of Izuna's head, her long dark hair running loose over her shoulders, covering her Squall's insignia. Sasha's peek outlasted its welcome, and as a result, she lagged behind Squall Ren. Even after running to get back by Ren's side, she struggled to keep up with his pace. She felt an urge to talk to him, to stay with him as long as possible, all through the night if she could. She had known Squall Ren as a dark brooding youth, and she had grown fond of it. The sudden arrival of his nemesis had been almost like a chemical reaction; he seemed taller, faster, stronger, leaner, meaner. Sasha's attraction to her senior officer grew a hundredfold. Ranks, situation, and Ren's consent became a blur. She wanted to lunge at Ren, pin him to the floor, rip his military uniform off, and kiss him to the blood.

In her fantasy, Ren kissed her back, and his long, thin fingers ran along her thighs, grabbing her by the waist and violently pulling down her skinsuit. His manhood would be erect, bursting with desire for her. She would spit on it before impaling herself and riding her Squall to orgasm, right there in the open, on this circular corridor linking the dormitories to the main dome of the station. Eventually, passersby would barge in. They would stop, exchanging consternated murmurs with each other, and Ren's lascivious hands would cup her breasts and expose her tits to the onlookers, and they would lust over her, over them, burning with the desire to join them, but not daring to make a move or say a word, pinned by fear, afraid they would not be up to the task; poor lovers lusting over the passionate embrace of two uninhibited souls consuming each other.

Sasha's fantasy was without release. Ren reached his quarters without having to fight her off or give in to Sasha's incandescent passion.

"Goodbye, Sanjo," he said at the door, facing away. "You may wake me up at five hundred hours."

Ren stepped inside his chambers. Sasha rushed to grab him by the arm before it was too late, before he slipped between her fingers.

"Wait. What if I... spent the night. With you?" Her upper lip quivered, and her smile lines drifted in and out of existence, as she moved her lips frenetically, unable to hide her doubt and apprehension of Ren's answer.

He gazed strangely upon her. In the dimness of the dark quarters, she almost didn't recognize the man standing before her. He looked at her without saying a word, her hand still on his forearm.

As if to stabilize herself and muster her courage to go through with her offer, she pressed a finger over her lips to keep her smile lines folded. "I could help you relax."

"No."

He brushed her arm away, and the chamber's door closed behind him, cutting Sasha off from her night sun. The darkness englobed her; the finger went down, her lips collapsed, and she became livid and bland like a kabuki mask. She soon felt her body poked by the minions of shame with their debilitating spears. She was deflated, the passion leaking out of her body through a thousand micro-holes. The walk back to her own quarters was a slog; she felt heavy, as if she were dragging an iron chain and ball respectively named anger and resentment.

WHEN REN WOKE up in the middle of the night, the blinds were open, and he spent a long minute observing the amber planet dancing before his eyes. He forgot its name, and for a while, until his mind cleared, he couldn't even remember where he was—which quadrant, which system, which space station. All he saw, all he knew, was her face. And her sword. And her name. Squall Miura. Miura Izuna. Izuna.

"This is the day."

When he got up, he had the certitude that this day would mark the end and the beginning of a new chapter in his life. Today he was fighting Izuna again, and this time, there would be no holding back.

At five hundred hours, Sanj0 Tsyukova came alone to give him the arranged location of their duel. There was a space corridor in construction off the edge of the third dome that could safely be used without being disturbed. Squall Miura had already been informed, and she was satisfied with it.

Ren did ten minutes of stretches before leaving his quarters. He arrived at the space corridor minutes before six. A dozen people were present, witnesses for each side. Sasha was part of a group of four, leaning against a metallic arch, her attention absorbed by the stars and traveling spaceships on the horizon. From this side of the station, the amber planet could not be seen. Neither Ren nor Sasha made an effort to greet each other. In this instant, nothing existed in the universe for Ren but Izuna.

She arrived at six hundred hours on the dot. It was almost as if she had been waiting outside the corridor for her cue, like a performer behind a red curtain. Izuna walked in, her movements deft and slender. She looked at no one, spoke to no one. Without ceremony, she drew her katana and adopted a dueling stance in the center of the corridor. No ceremony was needed. All the witnesses distanced themselves from the duelists. Ren stretched his fighting wrist one last time before unsheathing his sword.

The duelists were in position. This time, a witness counted down from 10, and the fight was on.

. . .

THERE WAS to be no observation round. The katanas were whooshing through the air and colliding with deafening *clunk*s before anyone realized the rules hadn't been laid out. Neither duelist seemed concerned; they battled as if everything had been convened. First blood, second blood, death: only the duelists knew how far this duel would go.

Early on, it was evident that Izuna had the upper hand. She used a minimalist approach, swinging short and dodging close. Her body was barely moving, but Ren's attacks were easily deflected or avoided. Twice, she opened a small window for a risky counter, but instead she readjusted her stance to defend the next strike.

After a full minute of relentless attack, Ren found himself already searching for his second breath. Izuna had kept her mouth closed the entire fight, breathing only through her nose.

You're trying to tire me like I'm some big hunk dumbwit, thought Ren, backstepping to put a good 10 paces between each sword. *I won't play that game.* Ren observed her, already finding himself on the back foot, trying to outsmart her. He waited, readying his defense, willing to be on the receiving end of blows, but Izuna did not come. She observed him, sword at waist level, two-handed. She hardly broke a sweat.

Come on, you've got more for me. Give it to me, Izuna thought, eyes locked on her opponent, refusing to move an inch forward, sticking to her strategy. Ren stood by, and so the duel came to a standstill, swords still drawn toward one another, sweaty hands clenched around their hilts. Ren allowed himself to breathe heavily, perhaps overdoing it to lure Izuna into thinking he had spent more energy than he actually had.

A murmur ran through the witnesses. There were questions whether the fight had come to a premature end, without any blows connecting. Sasha knew better. Her eyes were riveted on her Squall. She expected the first hit to come from Ren, while alternately he mused over Izuna's discipline and skills. Her footwork had been excellent, her sword movements scarce but stable. She was a tall and thin woman who exhibited tremendous power for her frame, although Sasha believed that, in a traditional samurai's sword fight, strength was not a dominant factor.

It's all about discipline. And clairvoyance, isn't it? I know few fighters more disciplined and cool-headed than Squall Ren, but this Izuna is certainly giving him a fair run for his money.

Silence filled the corridor. Outside the dome, three spaceships were approaching the station, unaware of the deadly duel it hosted. The red beams of the amber planet tinted the duelists in red, covering their panting bodies with a mantle of mysticism. They were two samurais on a space station billions of miles away from the land of the rising sun, reloading their chakras in a Japanese standoff.

Ren was indeed the one to break this respite. After stabilizing his breathing, he broke his fighting wrist to draw the sign of the tanuki with his katana, then punctuated it with a yell from the depths of his lungs, followed by a stabbing charge. Two steps before closing the distance with Izuna, he lowered his sword and slid onto the floor. Izuna had already readied a parry for his charging attack, but Ren's sudden shift unsettled her. She spread her legs wide and flicked her sword from side to side, not knowing where to position her arm.

Is he readying a vertical attack or is this still a stab? Izuna had to think quickly. Ren pushed with his back foot and lunged his arms into an ascending stab. Blade facing down, the straight position of Ren's katana gave his attack away. Izuna anticipated his movement just in time to shift her body weight to the left and counter and deflect Ren's stab with her sword. She found herself in a less-than-ideal position, on the back foot, fighting arm folded before her chest, at the mercy of a swift follow-up attack. Her years of training and close combat came into play. Instead of relying solely on her footwork and her sword to defend herself, she went on the attack herself, not with her blade but with her left fist. She punched Ren in the jaw and made him topple before he connected with his next attack.

Again, Izuna opened herself a countering window, but reason told her to step back and reset the balance.

This is a game of patience, she told herself, as if she needed a reminder of her pre-duel tactics.

She put her right foot behind her and leaned on its toes, leaving her left foot light on the ground. Ren rushed to hit her and missed repeatedly, Izuna slipping through his katana like running water, yet barely moving from her initial position and not once attacking. When Ren's arm tired and his movement slowed, a window big enough to try a sword stab occurred— but instead of attempting to slash through Ren's skin, Izuna poked his pride by punching him a second time. This time, she hit his neck. Ren stumbled and almost fell on his ass, and she saw in his mad dog eyes that all reason was gone. Now he lunged at her without brakes, without care, swinging wide, missing, his pre-emptive defense lagging.

At the first wide swing, Izuna kicked his ankle without strength, just to poke fun at him, throwing a last hefty log on an incandescent fire. Ren hit her with all his strength, forcing Izuna into two spectacular parries, before she bobbed under his sword and landed her first real attack of this duel. The point of her katana entered Ren's flesh at his inner left thigh and came out the other side. Ren roared in pain, and instead of swinging at her or collapsing under the duress of the injury, he head-butted Izuna. She stumbled backwards and almost lost hold of her sword stuck through Ren's thigh. To prevent her from removing the blade in a corkscrew, thus risking permanent mutilation of his leg, Ren pressed his hand around Izuna's hand holding the sword and pushed the blade out of his flesh. Blood spurted out of the wound. Enraged, he charged into another combo, but his injury made his movement gauche and slow.

Already Izuna dodged his blows without much effort. Now, with the duel already won, Izuna toyed with Ren. She easily dodged and countered, poking at his foot, stabbing his abdomen, twice. He refused to yield and roared in pain three more times before rolling on the floor and letting go of his katana. Sasha threw herself at him.

The duel was over. Ren was covered in blood. He had two abdominal cuts, a perforated thigh, and one of his toes hung by a thread.

Only now that the fight was over did Izuna allow herself to show any fatigue. Her lips split open, and she gasped for air as if she had been swimming underwater during the entire duel. Her body collapsed on itself, and she seemed hurt, although Ren had not connected any blows.

Sasha broke from the witness line to throw herself at Ren's rescue. Izuna watched the red haired officer running her trembling hands over Ren's wounds.

"He'll need stitches," she said to Sasha and the other witness kneeling at Ren's side for assistance. "You'd better patch him well. I'll…" Her sentence remained in the air. She left the battle arena without finishing her thought.

REN AND IZUNA'S first duel in space had been a one-sided affair that would leave indelible marks on Ren, physically and psychologically.

Instead of declaring himself unfit for service, Ren asked Central Command for two weeks' leave with immediate effect, which were granted with no questions asked. Whether Central Command knew about his duel with Izuna and whether they cared or not, Ren ignored it, but his gut feeling told him to keep it under cover. He wouldn't deny battling with a fellow officer if Central Command enquired, but he wouldn't volunteer the information. So, he took his leave and spent it in the medical care of the station's doc unit.

The station's surgeon successfully sewed his toe back in place and mended the hole in his leg. The slashes on his torso were wrapped up and fast-healed with the adequate sprays. Ren only had to stay still for a couple of days and refrain from laughing or sneezing. The leg wound took the full extent of his time off to heal. It left him with negligible scars on each side of his thigh which, if anything, brought more character to his thin and rather hairless body. Alas, Ren's mobility post-surgery was impacted. His leg felt heavy and stiff when he walked, let alone tried to run.

"With a series of regular exercises, you will regain ninety-five percent of your leg's mobility," the doctor said one morning.

"Five percent? I'm going to lose five percent mobility?"

The doctor unearthed his gaze from his med-pad. He observed his patient with his thin, dark eyes; he was probably a Mongol or a native of the Russian steppes. His demeanor was calm and soothing. Without making a noise, he put the med-pad away, rattled his throat, and looked beyond the insignia and rank of the man in front of him.

"Such is the nature of things, my Squall. I am sorry. We age, we battle, we tire, we get hurt. And, if we survive, our bodies pay the price."

Ren stared down at his leg, rubbing his thigh around the injury as if it could alter the healing's outcome.

"I've not treated or known many soldiers who have gone past the age of..." the doctor leaned on his med-pad to look up a figure "...thirty without their share of life-reducing injuries," he said, slapping his own thigh noiselessly, as if this would make it easier for Ren to accept the permanent loss of his faculties. "A hundred years ago," he continued, "you would have limped the rest of your life. Three hundred years ago, a bad surgeon might have amputated your leg."

"If I understand you well, I've suffered this leg wound one or two centuries too early to fully recover from it."

The doc cracked a laugh that he immediately repressed. "It's... not entirely wrong. Who knows? No one can see the future. And these days, with all these scientific discoveries being made at the Red Institute, who really knows? We live in fast and strange times. Today I am telling you that with the best of our scientific knowledge, you will regain ninety-five percent of your leg. Tomorrow, the Red Fleet might make a trade with the Huuri or the Cykens or some new undiscovered species and we might not only be able to fully restore your leg movement but enhance it. This is the nerve of this war, both frightening and wonderful in equal measures."

With his talk of scientific progress, the doctor almost took Ren away from his own worries. The good nature and enthusiasm of the man were communicable.

"Is this why you are serving on a medical outpost so far from Earth?"

This attempt at personalization in the doctor–patient rapport triggered a shift of attitude from the doc. He reached inside a drawer of his desk, leaning vulgarly on his chair. There were multiple clinks of glasses before the doctor took out two shot glasses and filled them from a bottle without a label, containing a brownish liquid with yellow reflections.

"I suppose, yes. Here, my Squall," he said, offering Ren a shot. They toasted without words and drank up. The alcohol was strong enough to momentarily tear their faces apart like a crinkled sheet of paper.

"Oumph, this doesn't taste like the regular stuff."

"It's artisanal. An old childhood friend makes it, from back home."

"What did you say your name was, doctor?"

"Bagherabakhan. You may call me Doc Baghera, I'm not fussy about appellations."

"And you're from? Kazakhstan?"

"Partly, yes. A small part. My family is from all over the place. We've got Kazakhstan, Tajikistan, Kyrgystan. And some distant cousins in Mongolia, too."

"That's a world away from the island I grew up on, in Hokkaido."

"And yet, you and I serve under the same banner, for the common and greatest cause of them all. Saving and protecting the human race. Isn't this wonderful?"

"Is this what we're doing?" Ren asked sardonically. "I thought we were out there to expand our territory and consolidate our domination in this Galaxy."

The doctor laughed joyously and poured out two new shots.

"I'm a physician, a conservator. I think minimalist, seeing only what has been achieved. You are a Squall, the finest soldier of our army, you think conquest and gain." Doc Baghera grinned widely. "Each of us is in its place, the human race can rest easy. Everything is in its right place."

"The right place, eh?" Ren mused, asking for a refill. "Don't you think, doctor — and I'm saying this because we are on a forefront battle station — don't you think that sometimes... we are... how can I say it? Too much in our right place?"

Before answering, the doctor clinked glasses with Ren and drank up. He instantly shook his head like a mad dog as the glass came down.

"You mean, too *restricted*? Perhaps. I don't know, it's not something that bothers me. I like boundaries. In science, it's important to know what we're up against versus where we came from. For example, with your leg, the quadriceps muscle and the femur have been touched; at present you're at forty percent mobility. This is where we start from. And with our current medical knowledge and the facilities on this station, I know I can help you recover fifty-five percent more of your leg mobility. Those are restrictions. I am fine with it. I find limitations comforting. This is what I'm up against. It's been done before, I have the tools to get it done, I can do it. And I know that a hundred years ago, you'd have walked with a limp for your entire life."

"And four hundred years ago, I would have lost a leg. Okay, I've heard you, but… what if I don't find those boundaries comforting? What if going from mission to mission and not knowing what I'm accomplishing is boring me to death?"

"Then I suggest you see a therapist." The way Doc Baghera tipped his glass toward Ren proved he was partly joking.

"I am serious, doctor. It's not just boredom, it's a kind of suppressed anger. I feel…" He lifted his empty glass abruptly. "Please, could you… could I have another?"

The doctor filled his glass with so much enthusiasm that he spilled alcohol on Ren's leg. The Squall wiped off his leg with the back of his hand and licked his fingers. He winced and groaned upon finishing his fourth shot.

"What I mean is…" Ren knew his speech was losing cohesion, but the doctor seemed to pay it no mind. He tried his darnedest to organize his thoughts. "I'm out there, running errands, leading battalions into battle, doing the dirty work, delivering arrest warrants upon unsuspecting Sanjos and Domions. I… there is no I, that's the thing. Where is it? Where is the *I* in me?"

"Where is the *I*?"

"Doc… Baghera. We've been talking for twenty minutes. We've gone way past the boundaries of the patient–physician relationship, yet you've not called me by my name once. Wherever I go, I see people's eyes stopping at my collar, reading my Squall insignia and bowing their heads. For them, for everyone, I am just a Squall. A Squall with no name."

"Good soldiers pay you respect. Isn't this one of the reasons people rise in the ranks? Respect?"

"I couldn't care less about respect. I'm not in it for the glory or the pride. I'm in this for… I don't know. I don't think I know anymore. But I knew then. When I saw her. Squall Miura. I knew instantly. I assume you know by now; she is the one who did this to me. She's the one who took five percent of my life away. But she took much more, and she can give me much more too. You see, doctor," he said grabbing the doc's arm, and squeezing his wrist between his index and major fingers like a crab clawing, "when I saw her, I knew instantly I was going to fight her. Because I wanted it. Me. Not Central Command, not etiquette or pride. Fighting her was my own choice. And I can't…" His voice broke. "… remember the last time I did something I wanted." Ren let go of the doc's arm, his voice deflated, as if all strength had left his body. "That's why I dueled her."

"And that's why you now have this wound."

"That's right." Ren chuckled. The doctor winced, not knowing if he should join in or not. "So, in the end, that five percent doesn't look too bad, eh?"

Despite all the battles and all his duels with Izuna, this was the first time he'd been seriously injured. This defeat would prove to be a life-defining milestone. Ren was too clouded by his leg wound and its lasting effects to recognize all the tiny changes that operated in his persona while in recovery. The amber light of the red planet near the station attracted his eyes beyond his reckoning; several times Ren was caught spacing out, observing the red planet through one of the station windows. He spent more time at the dining table, taking the time to properly dip his guzscha into his green tea. He began reading again, losing himself in *The Way of the Leaf*, the great autobiography of Jun Atsuki, the post-modern samurai. He changed up his training routine. In appearance it seemed to be because of his leg injury, but in essence it was much more. New techniques and exercises were incorporated into his daily practice.

The memory of how he had lost his last duel was vivid in his mind. The way Izuna had led her defense, taunting him, evading all his attacks with a deft economy of movement; it had been inspiring. For years, Ren had been content with his sword-fighting abilities. He had hit a plateau because he was satisfied with his skill set, and he had every reason to be so. His katana led him to many victorious battles and helped him rise to the rank of Squall. He had no reason to reconsider his practice routine. Izuna had changed that. When she bested him, she exposed his shortcomings. She had gotten better since their very first duel, and so could he. One thing he overlooked, though, was how much calmer she had been during their last duel, especially compared to their first duel in the Ahktokhi canyon.

On the eve of the duel, Ren had refused Sasha's offer of companionship. He had been harsh and insensitive to her. Blinded by Izuna's aura, Sasha meant little to nothing to Ren. Now that he had lost and Izuna was out of the picture, having departed from the station the next day, Sasha radiated a new light.

Now that he was recovering in his quarters, Ren welcomed her by his side; she who had been the first one to lunge at his feet when the sword fell out of his hand. It had felt good then to have someone care for him when he was at his lowest, bleeding profusely, abdicating his supremacy over his long-term enemy, Izuna. And although he had wanted to remain alone the first night out of the infirmary, he had not been able to deny Sasha's offer of company for long. Together they sat in the dark, taking slow sips out of a whiskey tumbler. Sometimes they talked, exchanging a few sentences and letting the conversation dry up without experiencing the awkwardness of silence. Occasionally, Ren winced after the tiniest movements. Even shifting his body from one side of the chair to the other was painful. Sasha lay in a lounge chair by his side, her foot hanging off the chair, marking the time with regular movements, like a pendulum.

A few directed questions led Sasha to tell Ren what it was like growing up in a fishing village outside Nizhny Novgorod. Sasha was good at telling stories and building a clear image in her listener's mind. Closing his eyes to better immerse himself in her tale, Ren saw himself holding a rod, standing knee deep in the Volga River. The water was freezing, even though his quarters were warm. Ren felt a chill running through his spine — the long arm of Russian autumn nights. As Sasha hooked a sturgeon and detailed her battle to bring it ashore, Ren's lips moved in spite of himself, forming words of encouragement, silently cheering on the 12-year-old Sasha from a million light-years away.

Before the story was over, Ren was asleep. Sasha felt she should excuse herself discreetly and get back to her own quarters, where she would battle sleep against the concerto of 11 other Sanjos snoring in unison. As unappealing as this option was, Sasha knew it was the right thing to do; her Squall's hospitality had only been extended to a degree. Yet, Sasha being Sasha, she did what she wanted and not what she should. So she stayed. Whatever would happen in the morning, when Ren would find her by his side, she would face the consequences without fear.

He can't sleep in that chair all night — he'll wake up with a sore neck, thought Sasha, observing Ren's neck rocking against the inside wing of the chair.

Carefully placing her arm behind his back, and slipping the other under Ren's legs, Sasha lifted him off the chair without prompting his eyes to open. He grumbled but remained asleep. She delicately carried him to the bed. He was lighter than she'd imagined. She had no trouble putting him under the sheets. Then she lay by his side, over the covers, and closed her eyes.

At some point during the night, she felt Ren's manhood pressing against her hips. She searched his face in the darkness. His eyes were still closed, yet his hands were looking for her body.

Ren must be dreaming. Some kind of naughty dream.

After exploring her pelvis, Ren locked his hands around her hips and turned on his side to push his penis against her, even though he was nestled under the sheets while she was lying, fully clothed, over them. Without thinking, Sasha slipped out of his embrace, letting her body fall off the bed, then she lifted the sheets and slid under. She lowered Ren's pajama pants, just enough to expose his penis, then she began to masturbate him. Ren reacted with moans and wriggles. He winced and groaned too, certainly because those sudden body jerks brought him pain. She brought her lips close to his glans, stuck out her tongue, and lapped the tip of his penis with quick and powerful thrusts, like an animal drinking milk. When she felt Ren tensing up, ready to explode, she wrapped her lips around the corona of his penis and masturbated him arduously until he burst out and ejaculated down her throat.

The seal of sleep hadn't been broken, but Ren, post-ejaculation, shook his head, moaning in pain, slapping his chest as if he was stuck in a nightmare. Sasha pressed her warm hand against his forehead and lulled him to calmness with an old song from her childhood spent by the Volga. When he calmed down, she nestled her head under his armpit and wrapped herself under Ren's right arm. It was a warm and delicious night, the first of many.

Izuna and Ren wouldn't be separated for long. Two months after Ren had started re-education on his left leg, Central Command tasked him with the rescue of a scientific unit on Z Prima. It was enemy territory, densely populated, a very dangerous and important mission— one with a high probability of failure and death. For such suicidal missions, Central Command did not designate officers; it gathered all its suitable Squalls on a holo-conference, detailed the proceedings of the mission and the objectives, then asked for volunteers. Ren was a volunteer. He made his decision the moment he heard Squall Miura's name mentioned. She was part of the crew stranded on Z Prima, in some underground lab.

The mission brief was given by a Russian exarch of Central Command. Unlike most of the Central Command exarchs, who hid their faces behind their respective colored pedestal avatars, this exarch appeared in person. Her official name was Zeele Uv. "About nine months ago, we captured intel of a hidden Huuri research hub, deep in Cyken territory. The research hub is located in an underground facility built on Z Prima. Those of you who have visited the planet or the sector before would know Z Prima as sub-tech world, populated by a Mesolithic-equivalent array of civilizations. Somehow, the Huuri have built their ultra-secret research lab deep below the planet's surface without the Cyken or the local population becoming aware." She pronounced "Cyken" in the singular form, without the "s"; it was a rare occurrence that, at first, Ren found irritating. Most people on the battlefront referred to the alien race in the plural form. "Six weeks ago, a small infiltration unit led by Squall Miura landed on Z Prima, found the lab, and broke in. They now have the research hub under control, and the experiments the Huuri scientists were working on. We want that research. Unfortunately, as you would have guessed by the nature of this meeting, Squall Miura's unit's escape route has been cut off by the Cyken. Five weeks ago, the Cyken deployed mass troops on the Z Prima, all over the world. They are ransacking the planet. We suspect they have acquired intel of the Huuri research hub and are trying to excavate it. Based on their grand-scale activity on the planet, Central Command surmises that the Cyken are ignorant of the location of the research hub. We intend to keep it that way."

At this moment, a map of Z Prima appeared before them all. It was a four-continent planet with multiple islands. The map zoomed to a northern continent where a blue dot marked the research lab, and a red one marked the rescue unit landing area. Ren ignored the size of the planet, but the two dots appeared at least a hundred kilometers away from each other.

"The rescue team will land here, in this deserted snowy patch where there is no Cyken activity. It is 336 kilometers away from the research hub." As Zeele Uv said those words, a red dotted line drew itself on the map. It was a straight horizontal line that prompted a Squall on the conference to ask what was on everybody's mind.

"This is air distance. Does this mean we're to fly to the research hub and back?"

"No. Air transport will be picked up by Cyken units. For a Mesolithic world, ancient methods. The rescue will travel on foot with skyhorses pulling wooden-wheeled carriages. You will ride to the research hub, meet with Squall Miura's unit, secure their findings on the carriages, and ride back to the landing site, while protecting the research, of course. Under no circumstances you are to engage with the enemy within a fifty-kilometer radius of the research hub. Squall Miura's unit will meet you three kilometers away from the hub's entrance."

"Is the research more valuable than the units?" asked Ren, having developed a certain understanding of Central Command's orders.

The exarch answered a straight "yes," as if people's lives weren't in the balance.

"There will be three carriages. According to Squall Miura, that will be sufficient to bring back the findings. The priority is the repatriation of the research."

"What about the lab?" asked another Squall's hologram. "Are we to forsake it?"

"For now, yes. We need a unit to land on Z Prima, under the Cyken radar, meet with Squall Miura's unit, and bring back the research and as many soldiers as possible. You will be expected to die if it means saving the research."

"I volunteer my services," said Ren with determination.

"So do I," said another Squall's hologram, a burly man with small eyes that gave his massive stature a disconcerting frailty.

"And I," said another: a well-built woman named Yun, known to Ren. She had made an impression on him as a very acute and resilient soldier. She was both smart and physical, an inestimable ally for such a difficult mission.

IN THE END, only these two Squalls and Ren offered their services. As each was located at various spots in the Galaxy within a day's travel distance to Z Prima, Ren and the others were given five hours to select their teams and thirty hours to report to Vurimia Space Station. Although given the opportunity to pick any soldiers and officers to serve under his orders, Ren did not pick Sanjo Tsyukova, nor anybody else on Nena Station. After the holo-conference, he packed up his gear and registered passage to Vurimia. He didn't stop to say goodbye to Sasha. He did not even consider informing her of his departure, even though they had been sharing a bed for the last month.

Somehow, Sasha found out about Ren's mission and caught up with him just in time before his ship transport departed. She barged into the passenger compartment. She was disheveled, a lock of red hair falling before her eyes. The compartment was busy, heaving with agitation. She had to fight off the cumbersome luggage blocking half the hallway and the travelers getting into and out of their seats, sometimes standing upright in the center of passage. Sasha did not pull rank to open herself a path. Most of the travelers were Sanjos, and there were even a few Domions in the lot. She scouted each seat of each row as she worked her way toward Ren sitting in the back. He watched her, in silence, his emotions dominated by annoyance and apprehension. When she got near enough, he stood up and made his position known. The seat next to him was empty. She didn't sit; she leaned on it with her knee.

"You're leaving me."

It wasn't a question, but Ren answered it nonetheless.

"Yes. Central Command has a new mission for me."

"It is so urgent that you were leaving without saying goodbye. Weren't you going to kiss me goodbye?"

Everything about this situation annoyed Ren, Sasha's panicked state and the claims she made on his decision-making, the embarrassment of being forced into a personal conversation in a very public and crowded place, and somewhere deep down he was angry at himself for not having spared a single thought about Sasha, whom he knew deserved much better.

"No," he said with the same determination with which he had volunteered to the mad rescue of Izuna on Z Prima. "You should get off now. The ship is about to depart." And he looked away, feeling Sasha's body next to him turning to ice before breaking into a million shards. He felt all her rage and sadness washing over him. He swallowed it all and buried it. When she disembarked, he dared not look at her. He blamed himself for falling into the trap of a personal relationship, getting a chill just thinking about the ties and new obligations that it implied. *More duties are all I need, really? Stupid. I'm a fool*, he thought, and as the ship finally took off and put some distance between Sasha and himself, Ren battled with a feeling he could not explain. He felt thankful. Thankful to Izuna. But he could not tell why.

WINTER

The forty-seven Qibings under Ren's joint command dubbed Z Prima "Siberia's Hellish Sister." Of course, it was inaccurate, because not all of Z Prima was a frozen, icy patch of land with sub-zero temperatures. Much like Earth, this planet had a varied climate, temperate above the equator, scorching underneath, but Ren and his battalion would see nothing but snow, fog, hailstorms, and ice. Although the atmosphere was breathable, helmets had to be worn at all times to fight off the freezing wind that left cuts on the soldiers' lips, cheeks, and nostrils. Two kilometers into their trail, Ren, who thought he could brave the adverse conditions without his helmet, got a cut on his nose so thick it split his left nostril in two. For the rest of the mission, a whistling sound accompanied each of his exhalations.

Progressing with helmets continuously deployed was dangerous. It deprived the battalion of all forms of verbal communications, limiting the orders to sign and other hand gestures. The wind barely ever rescinded. Troops took turns sleeping inside one of the three carriages while others trailed on. The march never stopped.

Sometimes, for kilometers on end, a thick fog joined the ball of miseries. Single-file columns had to be doubled and the paces between each pair shortened. It was impossible to imagine anyone or anything living in these conditions. Yet, Ren saw traces of reptile life, droppings large as an egg, but not the tail of an animal.

On the third day, 110 kilometers from their landing site, the battalion stumbled upon a small village. They were careful to go around it, benefiting from the thick coat of fog that kept them invisible. Taking cover behind a patch of tall grass covered in snow, Ren gave in to his curiosity to observe life in the small village in Siberia's Hellish Sister. The locals were humanoids, huge in stature, thick of shoulder, their entire bodies covered in layers of rough-looking tissue. Six of them stood outside their houses. They took turns stamping on each other's backs. It was a bizarre spectacle, one whose code of comprehension was inaccessible to Ren.

The battalion pushed on; the villagers did not appear to notice them, and if they did, they bore no apparent weapons. The threat was minimal, although the maximum threat hanging over their heads was that they might alert the Cyken forces surrounding the planet. Fortunately, the battalion arrived at the meeting point, outside the secret research hub, without crossing paths with the Cykens. Ten days had passed. If the route designed by Central Command was enemy-free, it did not account for the harshness of the trek. Although the Qibings selected for this mission were battle-worn and competent, the 10 days of trekking, with an average of 42 kilometers per day on perilous terrain, took its toll on the troops. Those who suffered wind cuts on their faces at the beginning of the mission lamented that the wounds were not healing and the pain was still vivid. Two Qibings had sprained their ankles and spent the last two days on board the carriages.

On the eleventh day, the battalion made contact with Squall Miura's troops. Every Qibing helped load the secret tech aboard the three carriages. The wounded winced and grimaced in silence, watching their moving shelter being filled to the brim.

The first thing Izuna did upon seeing Ren and the other Squalls was to comment on the state of their rescue battalion. "Those Qibings look like they just lost a war. Trouble with the Cykens? Is the mission at risk?"

She did not acknowledge Ren's presence, but her fleeting eyes and the way she shunned her body away from him spoke a thousand words. There was an invisible force attracting Ren and Izuna but keeping them separated, unable to face each other. Just being in the presence of each other was exhausting and exhilarating, like two opposite magnets refusing to come to terms with one another.

Squall Magalev, the burly officer, told Izuna about their grueling trek, but he failed to garner any empathy from Izuna.

"*Baka*," she said between her teeth, before giving orders to load the carriages.

"What did you say?" Squall Magalev was crestfallen. Although the meaning of Izuna's word was unknown to him, he had received the insult as she intended it, like a slap. "What did she say? What did she call me?" he asked Ren.

Ren's instinct was to dismiss his rival's comment, but he decided against it. He owed nothing to her. If Izuna decided to light wildfires to and fro, he would certainly not be the one to put them out for her.

"She called you 'stupid'."

The Squall reacted with a long string of insults in his own language. Ren did not speak it but could easily understand the overall meaning.

Looks like you've made a new enemy, thought Ren,

watching Izuna climbing on the carriages. Without realizing it, Ren was smiling.

ON THE RETURN TREK, the Red Fleet battalion took a different route. One hundred kilometers in, a series of blue explosions lit up the horizon, on a rare patch of land not submerged by fog. In the absence of Squall Miura, who guarded the tail of the caravan, the decision was in the hands of the three Squalls leading the caravan: Ren, Yun, and Magalev.

"Cykens?"

"Must be. Who could they be fighting?" asked Squall Yun, to herself as much as to the Qibings and the Squalls leading the contingent. "They wouldn't use such force on locals. No one drops a bomb on a band of peasants with forks and sticks." A somber idea hit her. "I'm... I'm not great at orientation, but is this the direction to our dropping point? Could it be that the Cykens have found our ship?"

"No chance," said Magalev. "For one, our ship is camouflaged, and the Cykens have not yet broken into that tech. And for two, our destination is that way." He pointed north. His intervention relaxed his troops, but the respite was brief. Twelve days into this white inferno, their metabolisms were tired, and many Qibings were injured, hopping on one leg and hanging onto the carriages to pull their weight. Although the possibility of battle was clear to everyone's mind during the mission's briefing, hurting themselves against the harsh and unforgiving reality of Z Prima had morphed this trivial eventuality into a looming monster. As elite as those corps of Qibings and Squalls were, no soldier fought well with only 20 or 30 percent of their capacities.

"The damned fog has cleared. The one time in two weeks that we needed it, it's letting us down. If the Cykens do a flyover, they could spot us. We need to go. Away from them. We need to chase the fog."

Ren spoke without thinking and immediately regretted his words. "Maybe there have been battles all around us, and we just haven't seen it because of the fog. All along, it's been a blessing, not a curse."

Nervousness met his remark. Qibings reached for their gunblasters in a protective reflex. From the Qibings who had removed their helmet to join in the conversation, three Qibings moved up and quickly deployed their helmets back on. A Qibing Ren knew and esteemed as a solid soldier threw up on the carriage wheel.

"We need to chase the fog," Magalev reiterated.

Squall Yun was not receptive to that proposition. "The fog is east. We're going north."

"We're going east," said Ren feebly. Behind the lead carriage, the troops marching alongside the middle wagon got closer. "I'd say we go east," said Ren louder, calling for a vote.

The Qibings near those who hid behind their helmets tapped on their plastrons, gesturing for them to remove their helmets. Ren repeated his proposition and raised his hand. Immediately, five Qibings, including those who had lowered their helmets, raised their hands. Squall Magalev was next. Six voices joined in. The vote was won.

"We're going east. Qibing—" Ren called out a soldier marching back to his middle position. "—go inform the rear guard about our change of course." He hesitated, and before the Qibing was out of hearing range, he added, "Tell Squall Miura the decision was voted on."

Going east appeared to be the safe option, but it proved to be disastrous. For 30 kilometers the fog escaped the Red Fleet, and when Ren and the troops finally nestled back into its mantle, they found themselves going downhill on wobbly terrain. The caravan pushed on, at first glad to be going deeper out of sight from a possible aerial recon. The first doubts arose when the path narrowed, and the company found itself sandwiched between a steep cliff and a short fall. The wind still followed them, hitting them from the side, pushing their frail bodies and carriages against the cliff. Parts of the road were icy. The skyhorses pulling the three carriages hurled at their drivers, shaking their heads virulently until the company came to a stop.

Squall Yun lowered her helmet to call up for a brief chat. "What if this is a dead end? What if there is no way out?"

Ren looked up at the foggy sky and smelled the cold air. "We're still outdoors. As long as we're outside, we can use the skyhorses to fly us out of here."

"For one thing, I don't want us to do that," said Magalev.

"Nobody wants it. It will take us forever and it will be extremely risky. We'll have to harness all the skyhorses onto the same carriage and airlift them one at a time. Then we'll have to come back for each Qibing. This could take hours."

"This is definitely a terrible idea. Magalev, you have the tracker. How far are we from the ship?" Yun asked, the wind making her body shiver.

"We are… 341 kilometers away."

"Three hundred and forty? We passed the 320-mark before we took a detour. This is nonsense. This road is leading us nowhere, and fast. I say we turn back and recoup with our original route before we end up facing a wall one hundred kilometers in the wrong direction."

"I second that thought," said Izuna's voice, approaching from behind. "Mind telling me how we got ourselves stranded in this death trap?"

Yun welcomed this support with a wry smile. "Those

Squalls here, Magalev and Satoshi, still think that all roads lead to Rome."

The moment Izuna entered the conversation, Ren retreated and refused to take part, going as far as shifting his weight so he wouldn't have to make eye contact with his rival. Uncontrollably, he wrapped his fingers around the hilt of his katana, caressing the idea of drawing and slashing through Izuna's arrogance.

Before a decision was reached, snow fell on the immobilized caravan.

We do not belong here, was the thought on everyone's mind, but it was Magalev who voiced it. "How did we get stranded in this hellhole?"

Squall Yun reminded the stocky man of their prerogative. "Central Command orders the excavation of the Huuri tech, we execute it. This is the way the Red Fleet works, always has been."

"We're going to die here. Either frozen to death by this planet or blown to pieces by the Cykens' patrols."

"If we die, we die, Squall Magalev," said Izuna. "Not living right is much worse than death."

Magalev frowned at Izuna's patronizing attitude. He jumped off the carriage to defy her with his imposing stature. Instead of laughing it off, as Ren expected she would, Izuna took his threat very seriously by pushing her power leg back and reaching for her sword.

Squall Yun intervened. "Enough, you two. Fighting will lead us nowhere. We are in this mess together, we four and all our Qibings. We take down a vote. Everyone gather." She called out a Qibing who watched the altercation at a careful distance, gesturing for those who had kept their helmets up.

"I suggest we send two trackers ahead to scout the road ahead."

"No," said Izuna, breathing heavily as if she had just fought a duel with Magalev. "One scout should go up, check on the situation above us. If the coast is clear, I say we turn back and rejoin the original route."

"We'll lose a full day just to head back," opposed Yun.

"And we might waste more time and resources if we keep going the wrong way. Listen." Izuna steadied herself, pushing her katana back and concentrating on her breathing before continuing. "I understand your precaution in leading us down this ravine, but we can't push on in the wrong direction just out of fear. It's been over twenty hours since we've entered this fog. The Cykens might have cleared. We need to make sure of it and consider the option of trailing back."

Ren heard Izuna's suggestion, and despite his best efforts, he could find no fault with it. The troops were diminished beyond reason; they could not afford to gamble with this hazardous weather and the possibility of an extended trek. They had lost a day's walk, agreed, but it was better to concede this small loss than risking more energy and resources they could not spare. Already, Ren doubted most of the Qibings would make it back to the ship if they got back on track, wasted no more time, and steered clear of confrontations.

"I agree with Squall Miura," said Ren. "I say this one goes without a vote. And also," he added as he jumped off the carriage, leaving Yun alone in the driver's seat, "Qibings should take turns driving the carriages. The wounded go first."

Yun conceded the need for a change of structure, but she did not only agree to it; she added to the proposition. "Let's set camp. We'll gather the carriages to make a blockade against the wind. You three," she said, pointing at a group of

Qibings standing by, "go gather combustibles to make a fire. I order a six-hour rest stop."

"Then it's agreed," said Magalev. "I volunteer to track ahead."

"I'll scout the horizon," said Izuna in a manner that called for no argument.

Not understanding why, Ren felt deflated, almost disappointed not to get the opportunity to ride above the fog, alone with Izuna. They'd been reunited for three days now, and had barely said a word to each other. In fact, they had only spent a handful of minutes within hearing distance of each other. *It's the longest we've spent in the same vicinity without calling for a duel. We've done great at avoiding each other. We're almost great at being no one for each other. Or… we aren't. Perhaps we are only fooling ourselves. Perhaps they've all seen me shunning her and grabbing my katana? I'm only fooling myself, and even that, I cannot do well. I'd give the lore inside those three carriages and the lives of every one of those Qibings to be alone with her and feel her yield under my blows. Ah… that is something I can master. But this place, this situation; this is inhuman. We are rats, trapped in a cage with limited food and water reserves, our captors waiting at the gate for us to break out. The white hell.*

Squalls Ren and Yun kept camp while Magalev and a Qibing rode ahead and Izuna flew up. Just organizing the bonfire and the carriages to form a half-circle closing against the cliff took half an hour and a lot of effort. As soon as the fire took, Qibings dropped lifelessly to the icy ground, rubbing their shoulders and arms to warm up faster, not embarrassed by shame. The lack of decency struck and frightened Ren. He had seen it once before, on a mission that went astray and ended up with his entire regiment locked up in a

Cyken jail on Lerani. Ren and his troops spent 120 days in a dark cell below ground. By day 30, the first Qibings had died from hunger or from their wounds. Despair overtook the troops and dominated their morale. No matter what plan Ren and his most optimistic soldiers formed, the light had gone out in most of the Qibings' eyes. Most of them gave up and let themselves die. By day 50, 30 Qibings had died. Ren made it out with only six other soldiers. They were the ones who had kept faith and hope in the face of adversity.

The dark memories of this traumatic event were sealed in Ren's brain. Out there, by the bonfire sheltered by three wooden carriages, flashbacks of the underground prison cell hit Ren. Distressing behaviors repeated themselves before his eyes. Most Qibings rolled on the ground like animals, shivering, spitting, cursing in their native language, frozen tears embedded on their cheeks. If Ren asked them what they thought of their chances of survival, he knew exactly what they would say: *We're all going to die here*. That's what they would say. And some would go further and indulge themselves in a rant against the one Squall who had handpicked them for this suicide mission, because when hope goes, decency is lost, and respect follows.

"The chain of command is on the verge of collapse," Ren murmured in Yun's ear.

Instead of speaking without thinking, she looked up from her own pain and misery to scout the troops gathered around the fire. She counted the Qibings who sat quietly, mouths closed, patiently waiting and resting. There were seven of them. Incidentally or not, they were all sitting in the same corner of the camp, opposite the Squalls.

"I do not know any of those Qibings," said Yun, low enough so that only Ren could hear her.

"I do. Two of them, the two women leaning against the cliff, were my picks. Qibings Arhagusha and Metelakhan.

The one closest to us is Qibing Natalia. I didn't pick her, Magalev did, but she was with me on Lerani."

"Lerani?"

"My battalion got captured by the Cykens. We were left to die in a prison cell below ground. It took us four months to escape. She was one of the few who made it out. She's a great warrior, but that's why I didn't pick her for this outing. I knew full well the potential risks of our mission. I couldn't do it to her twice. No one deserves to visit hell twice in a single lifetime."

Yun was silent for a moment. With the use of a small stick, she scraped the dirt out of her shoes. She repeated the same movements again and again, in places where the dirt was long gone. *I guess it's her way of thinking. Get her body stuck in a loop on a menial task while the mind runs free.*

"So," she started, dismissing the stick with a flick of the fingers, "you've been there before. I haven't. What happens next?"

What happens next?

"I'm not sure you should know."

"I want to know."

"Okay. It's your choice. If, and I say 'if' with the greatest optimism, if there's no miracle ahead or above us that allows us to get back to the ship in time, I'd say ten days, max, then… hell won't be this planet anymore. Hell will become the others. You see all those Qibings sprawling on the floor? Their humanity shreds away with each slap and roll they do to warm themselves up. Soon, they will forget all about themselves. Their minds are slowly dying. All that will be left in them will be a demon I called 'the untamed and unloved animal'."

"Why?" asked Yun.

"Because it is the way it is. In those situations, the weak

mind dies first, and the body follows, but not without causing rampage."

"No. I meant—sorry—why is this hard? Why are we so cold? Our skinsuits are designed to resist the harshest of climates. We can ride through space without being cold. So why are we cold now? Why is this so hard?"

"Moisture," Ren answered, wiping a wet patch on his forearm. "And time. I'm no engineer or scientist. In space there is no moisture, no air resistance. And we rarely ride more than a half-day period. It's fine for our skinsuits. They can take it. Protect us. But we've been here for nearly two weeks now, with no chance to dry up. This fog, this dense mist all around us, is keeping our skinsuits wet at all times. That's where the cold comes from."

"This fog is both a blessing and a curse," said Yun. She opened her satchel and took out two food pastilles. She offered one to Ren.

"No," he said. "Cut one in half; we'll share it. It's time we thought about rationing."

"Right, you're right," said Yun, splitting the small pill into two unequal halves. She stared at the seven Qibings who so far had maintained their composure. "What about them? Should we tell them to ration their food and water supplies too?"

Ren leaned close to Yun's ear to make sure he wouldn't be heard, fully aware of how conspicuous they looked to the troops, two Squalls conversing quietly with each other. "From now onward, consider these seven Qibings the bulk of our battalion."

His words startled Yun, who froze, the smaller half of the food pastille hanging on her lips. She put it down and swallowed.

"You mean until the trackers and the scout come back?"

"Yes, count Izuna in. From now on, this is what we have

to work with. The injured crab," he started, feeling Squall Yun needed more convincing, "does not hesitate to sever his own impaired limbs to better run away from his predators and survive. This, before us, is the bonfire of the crab. Our mission is now to survive."

"What about the tech, inside those carriages?"

Ren did not expect the question. Conflict rose in him. He twisted his tongue inside his mouth seven times before he answered Yun. "Would… it make any difference, to us, you, me, Izuna, those Qibings, if we bring this tech back to Central Command? What do you think?"

"It might help us win the war?"

"What war? This isn't a war like one in the history books, with a clear catalyst to start the war and a great event to end it. This war started when our people first began space exploration. But it's not a war, not like we've known. It is a constant battle. At least, that's what I think. Trust me or don't, Yun. Neither of us will see the end of this war in our lifetime. So, yes. You're right. This tech might help the Red Fleet in this tri-species conflict. But then it might not. Either way, we, as individuals, will most likely never benefit from it, never hear, see, or experience the benefit of the tech locked inside those carriages."

"You're saying our lives matter more than the tech we're hauling? That's a direct violation of Central Command's directives for this mission."

"I'm saying, Yun, that if push comes to shove, there be will other chances for the Red Fleet to get hold of alien tech. But you and me, Izuna, Magalev, and all our troops, we only have one life. We only have one chance. One life. One. Think about it."

Yun pensively buried her head behind her knees, arms wrapped around her ankles. For a moment it seemed the conversation had come to its end. But one last thought disturbed Yun.

"Strange," she said. "You call Squall Miura by her first name, Izuna. I thought Japanese people only went on a first name basis when they reached an extreme intimacy. Was I told wrong?"

"No. You're right. Some best buddies remain on a last name basis for their entire lives. Squall... Miura, isn't my buddy, or a friend. She's my nemesis."

"Nemesis, eh? I guess that beats all intimacy levels. Nemesis," she repeated, as if weighing the meaning of the word and its implication. "Yet you've volunteered to join this mission. I... must be tired beyond reckoning. My brain is fried. I don't understand why anyone would risk his life to save a person he hates. It... doesn't add up to me."

"Are you asking me for an explanation? Waste no more breath, I don't have one. It's like the French philosopher and physicist Pascal said, 'The heart has its reasons which reason knows nothing of'."

IZUNA WAS BACK within the hour, just as Ren was dozing off. She was formal: the Cykens had tightened their chokehold on their position; going back on their tracks was not an option. Whether or not the Cykens' patrol was aware of the Red Fleet's presence, they were there, getting closer to their position. The only way was forward, if forward led anywhere. Now all the troops were hanging on to the trackers' findings.

Magalev and the Qibing came back five hours later. They were not riding but flying low, above the ravine rather than on the road. In this fog, they had almost missed the made-up camp, only the faint glow of the bonfire alerting them to their position.

Magalev was panting. "There's a path ahead that leads back up to the surface, but it's after a long detour."

"How much of a detour?" asked Izuna.

"Sixty, maybe eighty kilometers."

"That's two days' march," said Yun.

Ren winced. "In our current state, more like three."

"We have no choice; we push on," said Izuna, and immediately signaled the troops for departure. She was met with little opposition, although the Qibings moved about at a maddeningly slow pace. No amount of shouting or threats from Izuna sprung them out of their lethargic states. Izuna grew angry. Yun and Ren exchanged a conniving look that needed no words. *Most of the troops are gone. They are walking dead.*

All four Squalls helped harness the skyhorses back onto the carriages, and when each mount had finished drinking its fill of water, the caravan rode on. Magalev and the other tracker drove the lead carriage, while Yun and Ren stood by its side. Helmets went down, and the march went on.

From that point on, riding down the narrow slope alongside a cliff and a sharp fall whose depth was lost in a thick sheet of mist, the Red Fleet battalion shed numbers almost by the hour. Two Qibings didn't get up. They lay dead by the cooling embers of the bonfire. One refused to leave, her ankle sprained and her jaw frozen. Izuna shot her dead, a straight blast through the head. As the three-carriage caravan came down the long slope, some Qibings drifted toward the back, to the point of losing contact with the third carriage, even though the battalion walked almost at a snail's pace. No one gave the order to halt and wait for those left behind. Yun and Ren knew it was pointless, Izuna didn't care, and Magalev didn't see.

After a handful of kilometers of rolling hills, the path going up and down at various intervals, the battalion hit the dreaded climb, kicking off with a serious incline. As strong as the skyhorses were, the passengers and drivers had to get off the carriages and walk beside them. The fog had cleared in this area to uncover an endless climb along a blue icy wall touching the sky.

"From this point on, this goes up all the way," said Magalev.

"All right, Qibings," called Yun. "Everyone climbs at their own pace. We'll have a rest stop every four hours for thirty minutes. We wait for no one."

In response to those brutal words, Ren offered the only encouragements he could think of. "Remember to keep a steady cadence when climbing. Your legs are an engine working at a steady speed. If you break that motion, the engine breaks. Find your steady speed and don't stop. Don't stop until the four hours are up. Feed regularly, a quarter food pastille every hour and one water pastille every hour, even if you don't feel thirsty." Ren looked over his troops, knowing he would see some faces for the very last time. "All right? March on!"

THE THREE CARRIAGES set the tempo. For the first hour, most of the Qibings kept up with the lead carriage. When the battalion hit a steeper incline for a short patch of 200 meters, those who were trailing with their arms hanging below their knees, almost touching the ground, moved to the back of the third carriage before losing contact. Ren, Yun, Magalev, and the seven Qibings who had kept a cool head throughout this ordeal positioned themselves in between the wagons. Only one person was needed to lead the front carriage's skyhorses. The battalion took turns.

At the first break, Magalev counted the troops.

"Thirty-two," he said, straining to rid his voice of emotion. No one mentioned that they had been 61 upon regrouping with Izuna's regiment.

Only Yun dared a comment. "I see a handful of them still climbing behind. Maybe eight, perhaps more. Maybe we could extend our break time?"

"What's the point?" said Izuna. "If they can't catch us now, they won't catch us on the next break. We feed, and rest, in silence. In twenty-four minutes, we march on."

Everyone knew she was right. No one argued, but the Qibings and Ren were angry none the less.

"This is shit," he told Yun. "CC sent us here to die."

Izuna overheard Ren's rant. She faced him and, for the first time since they'd met on this planet, their eyes met.

"What's that, Squall Satoshi?" she asked with a taunting posture, daring him to openly critic Central Command before the troops.

Though usually of a calm and reserved nature, able to exercise great control over his nerves and speech, Ren lost the reins on the carriage of his thought-train just by having Izuna staring at him, openly defying him.

"I said fuck CC. Fuck Central Command. They send us on this special mission, behind Cyken lines, to recover some kind of special tech." His voice was getting progressively louder. Everyone around the camp listened, even those who had just made it up the ramp, panting, drooling sweat, licking their wounds, and manipulating their hurt ankles.

Ren pushed on, rightly thinking he had already said too much. "They know how hard and how important this mission is, yet they're not giving us the means to see it to term. What about skyhorses? Helmets with integrated communicators? Special thermal skinsuits? We've got all this, nicely stocked up in our stations. For whom? For what? Better people than us. People who matter more?"

"We've got skyhorses," said Yun, with a quivering voice.

"Shut up! Six skyhorses for sixty soldiers? That's a joke. And those skyhorses are only meant to pull the carriages. The tech, the tech, the tech!" He let out a large gasp of air, placing his hands on his hips, head staring down. For an instant, it looked like he was done with his rant. But he was only readying the one thing that should never be told. In Ren's mind he saw the image of a lit torch in his hand, ready to be thrown onto a bale of hay, but what he thought was more in line with the myth of Prometheus bringing fire to humanity, knowing full well the damnation he would suffer in return.

"Central Command told us—" He visualized the torch being thrown onto the bale of hay. "—that human lives were expendable for this mission."

Ren's declaration was met with consternation around the made-up camp. The air became heavy with anger drenched in desperation.

"We," Ren continued, because no one interrupted him, "are expendable. Us. Squalls. You, Qibings. We don't matter. None of us do. We soldiers fight on the field, armed only with our courage and our meager weapons, low-range gunblasters and swords, for some of us," he said, looking at Izuna like he had never looked at her. Understanding had replaced hatred. Izuna mirrored his emotion. "Central Command fights with blood. Us. Humans. We are their weapons. We don't matter to them. When we get broken, or lost, we simply get replaced. We are expendable. We are tools." His shoulders sagged; he exhaled deeply and watched the steam come out of his mouth in this freezing weather. "I… am tired of being a tool." Ren grabbed the harness strapping two skyhorses to the front carriage. "I've served humanity. I did my share for the Red Fleet. Now my duty is ended." He drew his katana and, in one swift movement, cut off the harness. Scared, the skyhorses jerked and ran a few paces ahead.

The three other Squalls had very different reactions to Ren's act of rebellion. Izuna simply watched her rival. Magalev shied away behind his raised hands. Yun stepped in to prevent him cutting off the harness of the second carriage. "What are you doing?"

"Let me through. I'm getting us out of here. Six of us will ride the skyhorses and fly to the ship. Then we'll come back to rescue the rest of the troops."

"What about the Cykens? Or did you forget about the thousands of Cykens out there?"

"The Cykens can—"

A shrill noise coming from the third carriage overthrew Ren and captivated his audience. A loud rumbling noise followed, and before anyone could measure what was really happening, they knew. The third carriage had just toppled down the ravine. The raucous sounds of wood cracking on the rock echoed from the misty valley below. Dark shadows rising from the cliff side appeared from the fog. They were hairless creatures, with four arms, dripping some kind of hot liquid that made a dent in the icy ground, covering their steps in fumes. There were dozens of them, going for the second carriage. A Qibing shot the first blast. Missed. Ren saw the desolation in the skyhorse nearest the cliff as a four-armed creature ripped off a chunk of its neck. The other skyhorse panicked, tried to take off, and busted Ren, who fell on his flank, momentarily knocked out. The second carriage was two meters up in the air when the creatures chewed on the skyhorse's wings and tore them away. The skyhorse fell with the carriage, onto its side, half on the ground, half standing above the vacuum of the fall below. The carriage weight dragged itself off the cliff and the skyhorse with it.

The two skyhorses freed by Ren screamed and flew off,

carrying no one on their backs, saving no one. Now the Qibings were shooting left and right above Ren's head, who was numb and dazed. Something grabbed at his ankle; a katana he knew well swooshed by his side, and suddenly the pressure around his leg ceased. He looked down. A large gray paw with three huge fingers and pointy foot-long nails was wrapped around his ankle. He shook it off and ran to safety, behind Izuna's back.

Above Izuna's shoulder, he could see three dozen of those creatures crawling toward the humans, some going for the last standing carriage. The Qibings frenetically shot the creatures and hit them, but they did not slow down.

"This is a sword fight, Satoshi," said Izuna in a very sobering voice that woke Ren and shook him into action. He tightened his grasp around the hilt of this katana and sprung to attack the nearest creature. Before he could close the distance and strike his enemy, Ren felt his kidney lighting up and bursting into flames. A Qibing had shot him in the back inadvertently, giving in to panic shooting, not accounting for their Squall's sword attack.

Ren dropped to one knee. The creature lunged at him. Izuna stepped in. The sword came down. Gray, warm blood splashed all over Ren's face and torso. It was viscous, sticky, and solidified very quickly, forming a half-mask on his face.

"Your skinsuit absorbed the blast; it's not pierced," said Izuna, pulling Ren up by the arm. "Get up."

Someone shouted orders to stop firing. Izuna echoed those orders. The skirmish became a blade and foot-long-nail fight. The Qibings who did not have blades, or didn't trust in their short knives or lack of skill, ran off—down the hill, because it was easier. Izuna charged at the creatures. Ren couldn't move his feet. So he made a stand, sword held with two hands at his waist, waiting for the creatures to come to him. He saw Squall Yun dying first. Her elbow-blades got stuck in a dying creature's torso. Three creatures swarmed her and turned her into a puzzle that would never be complete again.

The other Qibings didn't have greater fortune against the enemy. For each creature falling to its death, about three Qibings died. Ren killed two, with great difficulty. Izuna was slashing arms and nails away but was getting hurt too. She was covered in blood, gray and red, rigid and liquid.

Squall Magalev did his best to organize the troops. He got the Qibings to attack in a three-wave formation of four Qibings per line. At each assault, the first line lost two to three Qibings. Those were bad odds.

"Let's go. Run. Run!"

She wrapped Ren's arm around her shoulders and dragged him away from the conflict. Izuna and Ren, two of the most respected and esteemed Squalls of the Red Fleet, abandoned their battalion in the heat of battle. If any human lived through this conflict and made it out, they would be sure to report that Izuna and Ren deserted their troops in the face of danger. Not only that, but that Ren had caused the loss of the skyhorses after a subversive speech.

Ren knew there would be no turning back for him. In spite of his kidney burn, he did his best to match Izuna's pace up the climb. There was only forward now. Behind them were the Red Fleet and the creatures, some of which may be running after them. He didn't dare look back, but Izuna kept watch. Ahead of them, there were two highly trained skyhorses who did not flee from their riders but simply retreated to safety.

"We ride!"

The first skyhorse came willingly to Ren, perhaps recognizing the man who had freed it from the toil of pulling the carriage. Putting one arm around its neck, Ren forced his legs to wrap around the animal's back, but his feet had barely left the ground when a sharp burn immobilized him and made him sprawl against the skyhorse's flank. The kidney burn pinned him down.

"Put your arms around her and grab her hair." Izuna helped Ren onto his mount.

The move was painful; the skyhorse wriggled lightly. Ren spat blood onto her short cream hair, but he managed to sit himself on her back.

"I'm sorry," he told the animal, scraping the blood off her hair. There was some on the wings, too.

"No time," said Izuna, running to the other skyhorse and jumping onto its back without difficulty. Behind the mounted riders, three creatures crawled at a frightening speed toward them. Neither Ren nor Izuna gave them a chance to close the gap. They hit their respective skyhorses' flanks and rode away from the battle.

"Let's fly!" shouted Izuna before deploying her helmet.

Ren imitated her and signaled for his mount to deploy its wings. The two skyhorses rode off the path, taking their flight above the sharp fall and the river of fog. They gradually flew upward to reach the end of the cliff and get back onto ground level. Flying with their helmets on, neither Ren nor Izuna heard the Cyken ship sprouting through the clouds to lock on to their tails. The Cyken ship fired two shots. The first one missed Izuna's head by a hair; the second blasted through her skyhorse's neck and detached its head from its body. The dead animal, with its wings deployed at a flat ninety-degree angle, glided past Ren and Izuna was shooting at the ship. The Cykens shot another barrage, and this time they took aim at Ren. His skyhorse got hit in the rear; it died almost instantly. Instead of gracefully gliding through the air toward the ground, like the headless mount ridden by Izuna, Ren spiraled down like a helicopter hit in the tail.

Quick reflexes and a clear mind were Ren's greatest

assets. They had saved his life in the past; they were about to do it again. While struggling to maintain himself on the dead skyhorse, he unsheathed his sword, cut its left wing off with a swift strike, then let go of the animal's neck to hold on to the severed wing. Ren pushed with his legs to propel himself off his dead mount, and the battle with gravity began. He had to secure the wing over his head to act as a parachute before he crashed into the ground.

At first, he fell in a straight line, faster than the animal. The hard, icy ground grew closer at a rapid pace. He got the wing over his head, but the pain from his kidney weakened his right hand and made him lose his grip. Instead of softening his fall, the mishandling accelerated it. Thirty meters before ground level. Twenty-five and closing. Ren fought through the pain to attempt a second stabilization of his made-up parachute. The wing was fluttering all over the place. He got hold of something hard, and locked in, but pulled only feathers out. Twenty meters. One more desperate attempt. This time his hand got hold of the wing's arc. Fifteen meters. He used all his strength to pull the wing over his head like an umbrella. It worked. Ten meters. The air got under the wing and broke Ren's fall so suddenly and with so much force that the Squall let go of the wing and fell from a seven-meter height at a reduced pace. When his legs hit the ground, he heard a loud crash and felt the breaking of bones under his right knee.

The Cyken ship flew over him. It was a small courier with limited firepower. In fact, it hadn't followed its two barrages of shots with any other attack. It dumbly followed Izuna, whose mount had turned into a real glider, falling down in a straight line at a steady incline. Izuna lay flat on her back over the animal's loins. With a steady hand, she blasted the Cyken courier with focused and well-aimed shots.

Cyken couriers were green tear-shaped organic vehicles.

They were meant for light and fast travel within a planet's atmosphere. They were not made for battle. Therefore, their shields were designed for air resistance; they were easily broken. Three good shots in the same spot, right under the nacelle, was enough to set the courier aflame. It half-exploded in the air. The degradation hit Izuna's dead mount and broke its perfectly angled wings. Ren watched in the distance as both courier and Izuna crashed one after the other.

Half a minute of respite was all Ren indulged himself in. He needed to help Izuna and possibly fight off any Cyken survivors. He tried to get up on one leg, couldn't, reached for his sheath, and realized with terror that the katana wasn't inside its holder. In the panic of the fall, he had forgotten discarding the sword to grab the skyhorse's wing with both hands. His sword was lost.

The only weapons left were his gunblasters and his katana's sheath. He used the sheath as a crutch and equipped his power-gunblaster in his left hand. Guided only by the smoke of the burning engines, he limped on the ice. What he had estimated to be a few hundred meters from the crash site turned out to be almost three kilometers. On one leg, getting to the crash site took Ren an incredibly long time. Half a dozen times, he felt dizzy and almost passed out. Only the thought of Izuna needing his help kept him up and trudging.

The courier had crashed in the crescent of small rolling hill. Black smoke rose up and quickly lost itself among the generous mantle of low gray clouds. The ship still burned, but the fire was contained to the front carcass of the ship, as well as several pieces of debris sprayed around the crash site. A dark figure came out of the ship, long and lithe: Izuna. She left a trail of blood behind her, and red fingers imprinted on the ship's hull.

"They're all dead in there," she said, wiping spit off her mouth and replacing it instead by a thick smudge of blood.

Because she hadn't looked up from the icy ground to make eye contact with Ren upon exiting the wreck, Ren wasn't sure Izuna was aware of his presence. He called her name, softly, as if to lure a wounded predator—a very dangerous, wounded predator. "Miura. Miura." The way Izuna lifted her head and stiffly turned in his direction confirmed Ren's suspicions.

"Are you hurt?" he asked, already knowing the answer, but those were the only words he could come up with.

Instead of responding, Izuna pointed a lazy finger at the sheath Ren used to lean on. "Not as bad as you, it seems," she said. "Is your leg broken?"

"I think so. It certainly feels like it, but I'm no medic."

"It's funny," said Izuna with an expressionless smile. "Usually I enjoy seeing you wounded. But this time, I don't. I feel cheated that I wasn't the one who did that to you." Now she laughed without a sound, her shoulders jolting awkwardly.

"You laugh like a fool," said Ren. Contemplating the thin, dark killer standing before a ship on fire, blood dripping from her arms onto the unforgiving ice of this forsaken land, Ren had to concede he'd rarely seen a more beautiful vision. He made no effort to repress a smile.

"What's with you, Satoshi?"

"Nothing. I'm simply enjoying the moment."

"*Hen*," Izuna said. "To think that a millennium ago, in the days of the Bushido, we would both have had to commit seppuku for what we've done, abandoning our troops… that's the real beauty to enjoy."

"You don't believe in honor?"

Izuna answered his question by spitting blood at her feet. "Honor, *anata*, is what proud and bored people invented when their world extended as far the horizon as seen from their bedroom, and civilization was as large as the members of their family and the village folks. In other words, I leave honor to the ignorant, which neither you nor I are."

"*So desu*. So, now what? We're both half dead. We're lost. Without skyhorses. The tech is gone, and so is our regiment, most likely. Now what?"

"Now, we rest, Satoshi."

"*Maji de?*"

"Yes, really," Izuna confirmed, and the two rivals got together to form a bonfire around which they could mend their wounds.

HUMANITY'S biggest asset in the Galaxy War versus the Huuri and the Cykens was its capacity for adaptation. While the Huuri ceased functioning over a certain threshold of damage, and the Cykens, in their rebellious nature, were known to lose cohesion and easily give up, humans had the incredible capacity to probe the parameters of the new situation they faced and establish a new set of guidelines for survival and the proliferation of society. In the duelists' case, it was a society of two. Their limitations were their lack of mobility, Ren's leg being broken and Izuna's back wound needing healing. They therefore defined the extent of their new world to the perimeter around the bonfire, meters away from the Cyken shipwreck. Ren's katana was lost, but he could still use both hands to shoot any incoming enemies, humanoid or animal.

Food rations were brought together and distributed equally. On a third of a pastille a day, the pair had enough to last a full two weeks. Izuna and Ren went into survival mode, sleeping whenever possible, with an eye open for any possible intruders. They deployed their helmets to keep away from the cold and remained in their sleeping position for days. No one and nothing intruded on the rivals but windy snow and more icy snow. Occasionally, Izuna would get up to gather more wood and use her gunblaster to revive the bonfire's flame.

Five days passed in silence and waiting. Five days in the company of one's dearest enemy was a very long time.

Ren was the first to express pessimism about their situation. "I don't think we're going to make it," he told Izuna, signaling for her to lower her helmet, but she shook her head and refused. Silence was golden.

ON THE SIXTH DAY, Ren tried to get up, failed, and entered a new world of pain. Instead of healing, his injuries were deepening. This time Izuna lowered her helmet.

"If you don't get proper care for your bones, you might never walk correctly again."

"You're worried about the way I'm going to walk? I'm worried about *where* I'm going to walk, heaven or hell."

By way of an answer, Izuna broke a stick between her hands. As the wood cracked, so did her back vertebrae. Izuna could not refrain from wincing audibly.

"Are you all right?" asked Ren, already knowing the answer but asking nonetheless, in an attempt at care and gratitude.

"No. There's no point lying or putting on airs anymore. You can't walk, and with this hole in my back, I'm not going to make it very far on my own. We are doomed. How ironic, that we're going to die together, killed by nature, rather than by human will and proper human emotion. That," she spat, "really bugs me."

"There's nothing we can do. Nothing we can do." Ren brooded over the words, as if he could find a solution in their vocal repetition. He thought about his life, all the battles and hopeless situations he'd faced. He saw Sasha's grieving face when they had parted aboard the transport. He hadn't wanted to say goodbye to her. *How insensible. It's almost… inhumane. Inhumane? No, I won't die in misery. I won't die lying down in the snow.* And thus, carried by his thoughts, Ren grabbed his empty sword sheath and used it as a lever to help himself up. Izuna looked crestfallen.

"Come on, Izuna. Let's put an end to it, our way, the way we've lived our life. Let's do this right. One last duel, to the death."

Izuna did not need convincing. She got up, drew her sword, and buried its tip into the icy ground. "We'll use our blasters. The one who kills the other gets to die the samurai way, with my katana."

"Agreed," said Ren, and he thought about adding more parting words to his long-term rival but it seemed strange and out of character in their tumultuous relationship. So he checked his gunblaster and began his long walk away from the bonfire, going east. Izuna went in the opposite direction. When they both arrived at a standard shooting distance from each other, they turned to face one another for the very last time. They saluted. The clouds were so low over their heads, they felt they could almost touch them. The bonfire was dying meters off the Cyken shipwreck. Ren extended his shooting arm; Izuna did the same.

"On the count of ten," Izuna shouted, and they both counted together.

Just hearing the word "ten" sent rush of blood to Ren's head. "Nine," he counted, palpitations hammering his temples.

"Seven. Six. Five."

When they got to "three", the low roar of engines disrupted their count.

"What's… It's a ship. Something's coming."

Neither duelist could see the incoming flying craft, but its noise was easily recognizable as another Cyken courier, and it grew as the ship got closer.

"Run!" shouted Izuna.

Ren tried, but slipped and fell on his hands. "I can't." The ship was nearly above them but still hidden from view by the mantle of clouds.

"Then get on the ground and play dead," she said and ran with all her might to get inside the wreck, to hide from the incoming Cykens.

As the ship broke through the mantle of clouds, Izuna had just the time to find cover behind the wreck. Ren lay inert on the ground, his hand holding his gunblaster concealed underneath his stomach.

Ren waited, eyes closed, helmet down, listening to the sound of the Cykens landing their courier and alighting on the ground. He heard three distinct sets of footsteps. They had landed behind him, meaning he couldn't see them. They directed themselves toward the wreck where Izuna had set her trap. As they moved closer, with slow, careful steps, Ren heard one set of steps stopping while the other two pushed on. Someone said a word, and the two Cykens approaching the bonfire and the wreck exchanged a series of sentences. Then the third Cyken got to walking again. His footsteps resonated louder on the ground than the other two. *It's coming my way*. Ren tensed his hand around the gunblaster trigger before relaxing it, ready to aim and shoot the moment the Cyken loomed over him.

As ready as Ren was, he did not expect the Cyken to brutally kick him in the back of the head. Unable to control his surprise and pain, Ren rolled over, shouting and losing precious time to beat the Cyken to a draw. Three gunblasts fired before he got a chance to press the trigger. He heard them and shot at the Cyken, thinking its dying alien face would be the last thing he would ever see. The Cyken dropped dead, two holes through its chest. Ren, aside from a new headache and his existing injuries, was intact. It wasn't the kicking Cyken who had shot, but Izuna.

"Two headshots," Ren heard her say. "Those were not soldiers."

The two other Cykens lay dead, headless, at Izuna's feet. She towered over them, proud, filled with a new hope. She was glitteringly beautiful, her long dark hair floating in the rising wind, dried blood spread across her cheeks and mouth.

"Now we have a ship, and a way out," she said. She stepped over the dead Cykens and rushed as fast as she could to the ship. Ren hadn't moved an inch. He still pointed his smoking gunblaster at the Cyken. His focused attitude took the spring out of Izuna's step. She froze in her stride, hit by the remembrance of what they had been about to do before they both added three unnamed casualties to their tally of bodies.

"You still want to duel?" she asked, her voice exhibiting both calm and fear.

As if taken out of a reverie, Ren dropped his gunblaster and exhaled deeply. "Are you kidding? Let's get out of here."

They both took their place inside the tear-shaped ship. Izuna held the command. She had no problem getting the alien ship off the ground. Ren suspected it wasn't her first time piloting one those couriers.

As the ship whooshed into the clouds, Ren felt the adrenaline leave his body. "We'll duel again. But not today. Not today."

Izuna took the courier above the clouds and drove it to the landing site where the Red Fleet stealth ship would be waiting. She met neither Cyken patrols nor any sort of threat on the way, but a handful of featherless birds brave enough to face the sub-zero conditions. All seemed well as the courier approached its destination. Izuna had the time to cool her mind. She began establishing a strategy to explain the mission's monumental failure. Just as she was rejoicing that there were no other survivors who could have witnessed Ren's incendiary and rebellious speech followed by the abandonment of the troops, the courier reached the landing site and found… nothing. The ship was gone.

Not believing her eyes, hoping the stealth tech kept the ship hidden from sight, Izuna alighted and ran circles around the landing site. There she found footsteps, four people's worth, and further she found the exact place where the ship had been docked. There was no mistaking it: four deep crevasses in the snow marked the emplacement where the wheels would have been moored. The ship was gone. Somehow, some Qibings had survived the attack, reached the ship before them, and taken off.

Could it be Cykens? The question prompted Izuna to take a better look at the imprints of footsteps in the snow. All of them were standard sized, only differing by length. She stepped next to a footprint and watched with horror her own imprint matching the others. These were definitely Red Fleet issue.

Izuna's mind raced. At this instant, the sleeping man inside the Cyken courier was her only concern.

He's going to get court-martialed if we make it back. I can bullshit my way out of my premature escape from battle. I can claim I was being chased by a demon and got separated from the regiment, but I can't lie about Ren's dissident speech and actions.

Izuna got back inside the courier and watched the innocent sleep of her old rival. At that instant, she knew exactly what she had to do. Slowly, she drew her sword. "This is the end of the road for you."

Lowering herself onto her enemy, Izuna got hold of Ren's empty sheath and gifted him with her own sword. The sheath was too long for her katana, but it kept the blade secure enough.

"Consider it your parting gift from the Red Fleet, Squall Satoshi. Ren."

Bright lights and metallic clanking tore Ren from his deep sleep. For the first time in weeks, he wasn't cold, but his body ached all over—his head, his kidneys, his leg. The ceiling moved rapidly before his eyes, neon lights quickly succeeding one another, yet Ren did not feel his body move. It took him an instant to realize he was lying on a stretcher and comprehend he was being carried to a medical bay in a space station he did not recognize. No one was there with him; the stretcher was moving on auto through the thin crowds of strange-looking aliens. There were no uniforms in sight, only people in rags and grandiloquent frocks: pirates, merchants, survivors.

Before he reached the medical bay, Ren caught sight of an inscription on a wall: "Mesigna Station, EE."

A neutral space station.

Inside the medical bay, the doctor who greeted him was Cyken. They had feminine traits but a rugged voice. Cykens were known to be ambisexual and had the ability to shift their sex and appearance at will, yet Ren had never witnessed this change in a single Cyken. The Cyken doctor made no remark at his Red Fleet skinsuit and began working on his leg immediately. It didn't take him long to announce that they would have to break the leg again. As Ren had feared, the bone had healed in the wrong position. Then, without consideration for any level of pain or discomfort Ren was experiencing, the doctor virulently flicked him onto his belly to examine his kidney shot. Ren winced in pain. As soon as the doctor had finished cutting through the skin suit with a large antique-looking pair of scissors, they swore in their native language.

To Ren's surprise, the doctor spoke Russian—and good Russian; their accent was no worse than the standard Japanese Qibing's. "This is bad one. Need injections."

The doctor hadn't finished the sentence when they plunged a long syringe inside Ren's chargrilled kidneys.

"You're going to feel a bit dozy. This is standard Cyken treatment. Might be a bit strong for you."

"Wait, wait, wait. Have you ever cared for a human being before?"

"Of course. Many times, and they were all very…" The doctor flicked a small syringe before their eyes and virulently plunged it into Ren's ribs.

The doctor didn't bother finishing the sentence. Ren felt instantly drugged up, his mind and vision blurry. For the next hour, the doctor worked on him, Ren dropping in and out of consciousness.

At one point, when Ren was completely naked on the operating table, and the doctor was busy wiping something at the back of his head, Ren saw a vision of Izuna approaching.

"You're going to live," she said, with a hint of forced optimism.

"I…" was all Ren could muster.

"It's all right. How much do you remember?"

"E… everything. Why… are we not back?"

"You can't come back to the Red Fleet. Your career is over, Ren. After your speech and what you did on Pri—" Conscious of the doctor listening, Izuna cut herself short in time. "—over there, there is no way back for you. Not that I think you'll want to come back, after what you said."

"No." Ren hadn't had time to think about his future, but he knew his time with the Red Fleet was done.

"So here we are. After this many duels. I grant you freedom, like you so often granted mine. But I'm staying," she said, tapping her officer's pins. "I'll make amends. I've learned to love Central Command and understand them for who and what they are. No one is perfect, and sometimes order and injustice is what it takes to keep a civilization together. I understand that. The Red Fleet is where I belong."

Ren didn't respond. In fact, he had closed his eyes, and Izuna feared he had gone back to sleep. "I must go now," she said, grazing his shoulder. She picked up the sword she had donated to him and brought it before his eyes. "This is for you, Ren. My katana. I know you lost yours. You're going to need one wherever you're going, from now on."

"You're giving me your blade?"

"I used to feel lost under Central Command, and it made me angry, all the time. You've helped me contain my wrath and find my peace within the Red Fleet. This is my home, but this isn't yours. I hope, one day, you will find your home, wherever it may be. Goodbye, Ren."

The next time Ren flicked his eyelids, Izuna was gone. Her sword rested by his side, along with a small bag. Ren ran his fingers to grope its contents and guessed the shape of coins inside. A lot of coins. Enough to make a fresh start in life.

NEW SPRING

For five years, Squall Miura kept the truth about Ren's death on Z Prima hidden. After making her report, she was held for a very brief interrogation. She was never told why—the interrogator only asked her two questions—but she guessed some of the details in her report did not match with the other survivors of Z Prima, those who had come back with the Red Fleet stealth ship. She was asked if she'd heard Squall Satoshi Ren's slander against the Red Fleet. She told the interrogator that she had, and that she also saw him killed and taken down the ravine by one of the endemic creatures who had attacked the camp.

Her response satisfied the inquisitors, who released her without further questions. She wasn't asked again about Squall Ren, not until full five years later, when she sat at a meeting discussing the administration of a newly seized Huuri world. In front of her there was a Domion with fire-red hair and small chestnut eyes who stared at her the entire meeting. She didn't actually say a word herself, but her face expressed a boiling anger. When Izuna spoke, she was self-conscious, feeling the weight of the stranger's gaze upon her. It hampered her loquacity. Twice during the meeting, Izuna thought about confronting the Domion; twice she kept herself from making an outburst. Something about this woman echoed in her memory. She had seen her somewhere, in a difficult situation, but despite all her best efforts, she could not remember where.

"You're a liar," erupted the Domion, standing to face Izuna after the meeting, when the two women had stayed behind, locked in a staring contest. Immediately after she accused Izuna, the Domion's face shifted to a sorrowful tone. From aggressive, she now looked almost fragile.

Her vulnerability impacted Izuna, who took it upon herself not to react to the insult. "Do I know you? I feel like we've met somewhere, yet I can't place it. Have we served on a campaign together?"

"We haven't. I was one of Squall Satoshi Ren's seconds during your duel."

The mention of Ren's name threw Izuna off-balance. It was the name of a ghost—one she had started to forget. Izuna took a second to compose herself, readjusting her sitting position around the deserted meeting table. "I have fought many duels with Squall Satoshi. Excuse me if I cannot remember all his seconds."

"I was a second at your last-ever duel, about three months before Ren's *death*. If it was, in fact, your last-ever duel together. Who knows if you haven't lied about that, too?" As if the Domion was growing confident in the conversation, her last words were marked with a defiance and an insidious attack Izuna could not ignore.

"You stand there to accuse me of fallacy, yet I don't know your name."

Anger colored the Domion's face anew. "Do you? Am I that forgettable? We've met twice before, and I said my name when we started this meeting three hours ago."

"Sorry, I wasn't paying attention."

"You selfish bitch," the Domion said between her teeth. This new insult was enough to uncork the safety on Izuna's gunblaster, who sprang from her seat in a split second to hold the Domion at gunpoint.

The Domion remained calm, undisturbed, as if it was all part of a plan. Her cool unnerved Izuna, who could not find the right words to back up her actions.

"Yes, of course," said the Domion with a sneer. "You couldn't kill your worst enemy, but you expect me to believe you're going to shoot me in cold blood over a tiny little insult? Sorry," she said, standing up but keeping her hands free from weapons. "Given your past history, I don't buy it."

"Shut up!" The Domion's words angered Izuna, who was mesmerized by how quickly she had lost control over the situation. "What is your name, Domion? I am your commanding officer, answer me!"

"My name," shouted the Domion, matching Izuna's tone, "is Aleksandra Tsyukova. Ren Satoshi was my lover."

"Sasha Tsyukova?" Now Izuna was hit by flashes of the duel where she had maimed Ren's leg. This woman had been the first to throw herself at his rescue. "You're that red-haired woman who nursed him after our duel on the space station? I didn't know you were his partner, not that I care."

"Of course you didn't. You don't care about anything. You just take what you need and discard the rest without any concern for others. You took him away from me. Not once but twice. First when he answered your distress call from that damned planet. And then when you lied about his death."

"What did you say?"

"You lied about Ren's death! He's not dead, he never was! For five years, you robbed me of him. You stole all those tears from me, and all the days we could have been reunited."

"Nonsense. Squall Satoshi died on Z Prima. I saw him die with my own eyes."

"Lies, lies, lies!"

"Shut up! Stop attacking me, or I am going to hurt you."

"You've already done that. Don't you understand? You stole Ren from me." Anger deserted Sasha, and now she was on the verge of tears, her small eyes fringed by dozens of tiny wrinkles. "When I thought he died on Z Prima, I was devastated. But I understood, because it was a dangerous mission and only a few made it back. You made it back. The months that followed were difficult, but I got over it. I made myself a reason. He… we didn't have enough time together. He didn't love me as much as he cared for you and your stupid duels. Your feud got the best of him. I could understand that. It was stupid, and that killed him. The stupidity of his death is what truly helped me get over him. I got married two years ago, to a man who is nothing like Ren was. I don't love him, but I am comfortable with him. My life was comfortable. Until… until I heard about a Cyken prison break on the outskirts of Zigmut space. A prison called 'the Abyss', one of the Cykens' greatest incarceration facilities. Before this escape, no one had ever broken out of the Abyss. Yet, last month, five people did. They were all part of the same gang of misfits. One of the names on the prisoners' register was Satoshi Ren."

"What makes you think it was him? Do you know how many Japanese-born men are called Satoshi Ren? There are probably thousands of—"

Sasha popped up a hologram ball and threw it onto the table between Izuna and her. A hologram image of five individuals opened itself. It was a wanted poster with a tael sum under each face and name. Over the 8,000 figure was Satoshi Ren's name, and above it was the face of a man with long hair who looked incredibly like the Satoshi Ren they both knew.

"Tell me that's not him," said Sasha.

Izuna was crestfallen. She stared at the hologram of Ren with empty eyes. If she had wanted to lie in this instant, her eyes would have betrayed her.

"He's alive. Isn't he?" continued Sasha. "He never died on Z Prima, like you said he did. Did he? Tell me. I need to know. I've lived a lie long enough. Tell me…"

"I can't… tell you for sure if it's him. But… yes. Ren did not die on Z Prima." The revelation made Sasha collapse on herself. Izuna pushed on, resolute now to tell the Domion the entire truth, everything she knew. "We escaped together in a Cyken courier we stole. He couldn't come back to the Red Fleet. He would have been court-martialed. He was also very hurt. His arm was broken or something, he wasn't well, he needed urgent medical attention. So, I took him to a neutral space station and left him in the care of a doctor. I gave him my sword, and all the money I got from selling my gunblasters on the black market. I wanted him to be free. I have never seen or heard of him since then. I don't know what happened to him."

"Neither did I, but now I know," said Sasha. "And this changes everything. Everything." She made her way to the exit, leaving the hologram ball playing on the table. "You, Squall Miura, with all due respect, destroyed everything I have, for the second time in my life. If I was dumb enough, I would challenge you to a duel. And I would probably die, because you are a better duelist than I am. But I am a better person. I am better than that," Sasha said, her eyes sparkling with brittle confidence in herself.

"Yes," said Izuna, before Sasha walked away. "You're too comfortable to duel me. I understand it." Sasha sneered and stormed away. In her head, Izuna finished her sentence: *Satoshi understood it too.*

Izuna's eyes were riveted to the figures in the hologram.

Alongside her old rival's profile there were four others: two black men, one thin, one burly. Both were smiling. There was also a young Asian woman with pink and blue hair, very pretty, and a chubby Latino man, smiling too. Ren's wanted fee was the highest of the lot. Over the five heads, a title read: "Wanted: escaped convicts from the Raoke Gang."

"The Raoke Gang?" Izuna mused. "Is this it, Ren? The home you've been looking for? The Raoke Gang." A faint smile drew itself on her lips, and suddenly all the tension had evaporated. She was cool and relaxed. "Looks like a fun bunch."

THE END of *The Choice of Weapons*, the first entry in the Raoke Gang Series.

FROM THE AUTHOR

Dear Reader,

Thank you for reading my debut novella. I've come a long way from being a lonely child back in a French village with his head full of dreams and adventures; a child who failed English (as a second language) at his final school exam. To have people reading my work and hopefully enjoying the ride and taking something away from it truly fills me with joy.

Back in 2012, I took the decision to leave France and stop writing in French in order to find a bigger audience. I knew I was taking a big risk, that the transition was almost impossible to make and that writing in a second language would always put an invisible cap on my writing abilities. Every day I am honing my craft and my prose. I want to be the best writer I can be and break that invisible ceiling.

I've toiled for too many hours and sacrificed too much just to entertain a handful of people. My aim is to write unforgettable novels, filled with raw emotions, real people and incredible settings. The Choice of Weapons is right at the beginning of that journey. Like Ren, I've picked my weapons: to be an indie author writing in English. Now, I don't have a rival like Izuna to motivate me and save my life, but I am driven by a simple ambition: to become a great writer.

Whether or not I'll get there, I'll keep on giving my very best. But I won't make it on my own. I need you and all the help you are willing to offer. You can't write my stories for me (because I won't let you), but you can join my review team to help with the launch of future releases. You can became a beta reader to share your advice on plot points I am unsure about during the editing process. Or, simply, you can send me an email or reach out on social media to share your experience reading my books, or point out a mistake I've made on a promo post, a typo I've left in a book or a newsletter.

If you are willing to help me write more quality novels, the biggest impact you can have is to review my books on Goodreads and Amazon, and share the word about the Raoke Gang.

As a thank you, I am offering you a free Raoke Gang novelette. Download The Adventures of Dani Botswana and join my mailing list to stay up to date with the Raoke Gang's adventures.

Thank you for trusting me with your time and embarking on this amazing journey with me.

Affectionately yours,

Alex Valdiers

ACKNOWLEDGMENTS

Thank you to all the artists who have helped me bringing The Choice of Weapons to life: Luka Brico for the cover illustration, Dan Coxon for the copy-editing, Sarah Hart for the proofreading and consistency check, Elaine West and Joseph Paul Bernstein for beta-reading all my stories.

Most important of all, thank you to my wife Andrea for her time and understanding when the Raoke Gang and Bloodbreaker series consume so much of my time and energy.

Printed in Great Britain
by Amazon